MURDER IN ABSTRACT

A Charley Hall Mystery, Book 5

Brenda Gayle

Bowstring Books

Murder in Abstract
(A Charley Hall Mystery, Book 5)
by Brenda Gayle

Published Internationally by Bowstring Books
Ottawa, Ontario, Canada

EBOOK ISBN 978-1-7775824-0-1
PRINT ISBN 978-1-7775824-5-6

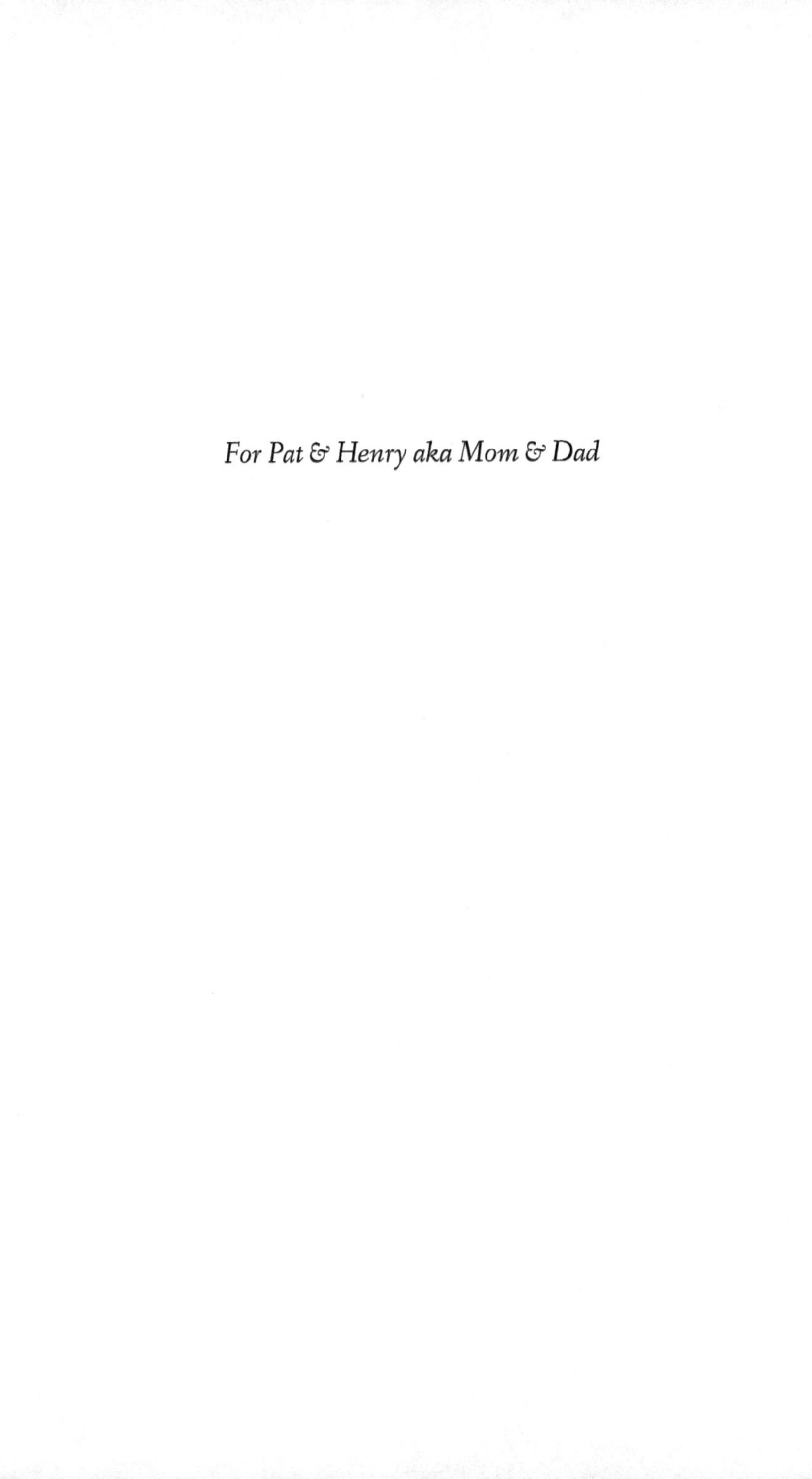

For Pat & Henry aka Mom & Dad

THERE IS an energy that pulses through a newsroom when a reporter catches a story. For a fraction of a second, time is suspended by the tension of anticipation. To the uninitiated, it goes unnoticed, but to the reporters in the pit, the jolt of a potential scoop sparks their own creativity, and they return to their typewriters with renewed vigour.

Charley Hall looked up from her desk in the corner of the *Kingston Tribune*'s newsroom to see which reporter had received the lucky break. Lester Pyne was on his feet, his pudgy face flushed with excitement. Not long ago she would have resented him for it, but she'd come to terms with ceding her place on the city beat to the World War II veteran. Her interest now was on transforming the women's pages from their traditional focus on fluff and finery to a serious instrument for societal change.

But that didn't mean she wasn't curious.

"Hey, Lester, what's cookin'?" she called to him.

He held up his hand to stall her while he answered his telephone.

She pushed back her chair and crossed the room to peer over his shoulder while he jotted down a name and address.

Senator Overstreet. King Street West.

Lester hung up the telephone. "A dead cop and some

stolen paintings," he said, stubbing out his cigarette in the overflowing ashtray on his desk. He brushed past her to grab his winter coat from the coat tree.

"Not the *Rouge et Jaune* collection?"

"The what?" He turned back to her.

"The *Rouge et Jaune*. I was there last night for the *vernissage.*"

"Verni—" Lester shook his head, confused.

"*Vernissage,*" John Sherman interrupted, stepping out of his office. It's a private showing before the actual exhibition which, if I remember correctly, was to be in Toronto, right?" The managing editor turned to Charley. "I thought Mrs. Overstreet cancelled it."

"Yes, a gallery in Toronto is—was—going to exhibit them," Charley replied. "In terms of last night's *vernissage,* though, I did get a message that Mrs. Overstreet was worried about the predicted snowstorm. Her home is only a few blocks from mine, so I went ahead anyway. Besides, I'd already booked Brownie and it was too late to try to get hold of him about any change of plans." Brownie was the *Trib*'s overworked photographer.

"So, it went ahead?"

"There weren't many people there, but yeah. I'm working on the article now."

"Okay. You go with Pyne, then." Sherman turned on his heel and returned to his office.

Lester deflated. "I don't know what just happened."

"Don't worry, I'm not going to steal your story," Charley assured him. "But if someone stole the *Rouge et Jaune* paintings, I need to add it to my article. You focus on the dead cop and I'll stick to the art angle, okay?"

"ARE YOU SURE WALKING IS FASTER?" Lester wheezed from the effort of trudging through the snowdrifts.

Charley didn't bother replying. The absence of vehicles braving the unploughed streets was her answer. Besides, it was a pretty direct thirty-minute walk south from the *Trib*'s office to the Overstreets' waterfront home.

Maybe you should try cutting back on the cigarettes.

She immediately regretted the uncharitable thought. Lester smoked like a chimney, but a lot of the war vets did. Besides, what harm was it really—especially when compared to some of the other vices the soldiers took up to deal with all they'd seen and done? Her own brother, Freddie, had been waging a battle with the bottle since his return.

The snowstorm may have arrived later than predicted last night, but when the flakes started coming down, they did so with a vengeance. Already there was a good five inches on the ground, and it didn't look like it was going to abate any time soon.

After rounding the corner and travelling less than a block along King Street, Charley turned and headed up a long driveway.

"Holy moly!" Lester said, quickening his pace to catch up. "And I thought the Bankses' place was swanky."

Charley squinted through the falling snow and tried to see the house through Lester's fresh perspective. The two-storey, pebble-cast stucco building had massive, centrally placed chimneys, cantilevered eaves, and evenly spaced windows of contrasting sizes. Its perfect symmetry, however, was marred by the single-storey wing tacked onto its eastern side.

"It was built in the middle of the last century by a fellow who'd been elected mayor of Kingston," she said.

"But because the house was technically outside city limits, he had to forfeit the office. Harold Overstreet bought it in the twenties before he was named to the Senate."

"How do you know all that?"

She shrugged, unwilling to go into her conflicted history with the Overstreet family. Well, not the entire family.

"How'd they beat us here?" Lester moaned and motioned to a group of men huddled together, several yards back from the enormous carriage porch that dominated the central front entrance. "I told you we should have—"

Charley kept walking. It didn't matter that reporters from the other news outlets had already arrived. It was obvious they hadn't been successful in getting any information from the police.

"Constable Marillo!" she called out. Several of the officers glanced over at her, but quickly returned to what they were doing.

One of the men disengaged himself from the group and came toward her, frowning. "Mrs. Hall, this is a surprise. I wouldn't think this would be of interest to readers of the women's pages."

"Did you get called in at the last minute?" she asked, nodding at his navy peacoat and jaunty fedora.

"You haven't heard? I'm a detective now."

"Congratulations. It's about time." Charley was genuinely pleased for him. Marillo had been with the police department for a long time and had more than paid his dues training ambitious young officers.

He took off his fedora and shook the snow off it. "Darn brim catches too much snow." He put the hat back on. "I do miss the uniform. It was much easier getting ready each morning, knowing what you were expected to wear. Now, the Missus feels she must give me a full inspection before I leave the house. I tell her I'm a grown man and can dress myself, but for some unknown reason, she thinks my appearance reflects on her."

"Well, you look very dapper, *Detective* Marillo. Your wife should be most proud."

"Thank you, Mrs. Hall. I shall tell her you said so." His head jerked up sharply and his lips tightened as if noticing something unpleasant. He took her arm and led her under the carriage porch.

Charley glanced back over her shoulder and watched a dejected Lester Pyne slink back to the group of reporters.

"Now, Mrs. Hall, why are you really here?"

Standing closer to the house, she could see what the police cruiser had hidden. Two uniformed officers and the medical examiner were hunched over a brownish mound by the east wing. "Is that the dead cop?" she asked.

"No comment. And if you keep stalling, I'll make you go stand with your *compadre* over there."

"I'm here about the stolen paintings. I was at the viewing last evening."

"You were?" Marillo reached into his pocket and withdrew a notepad and pencil. "What time was that? Who else was here?"

"Not so fast. I'll tell you what I know if you tell me what you know."

"That's not how this works."

"Look, I'm not on the city beat. The dead cop is Lester's story. I'm here to get information about the theft to flush out my article on the paintings. If you tell me what you know, I'll tell you everything I remember from last night. Heck, the *Trib* had a photographer here; I can even get you copies of the pictures he took."

"All right," Marillo conceded, although he didn't look

happy about it. "According to the housekeeper, two police officers arrived earlier this morning to pick up the paintings and take them to the art gallery in Toronto. As they were starting to load them into a white delivery truck, a blue truck arrived. There was some sort of altercation. One of the men from the white truck was killed and the men from the blue truck made off with the paintings."

Some sort of altercation? How many men in the blue truck?

Was Marillo being deliberately vague?

Charley looked along the driveway. She could make out the faint ridges where the tires from the two trucks had left a criss-crossed track. "What happened to the second cop? Did he go after them? In this weather, the blue truck couldn't have gone fast, or far, for that matter."

"Well, well, well, looks like the gang's all here," a familiar voice sang out in an unfamiliar jovial tone.

Charley whirled toward the entrance of the house as Mark Spadina sauntered over.

She hadn't seen the cop-turned-private-detective since Christmas Eve, although against her will he managed to sneak into her thoughts more often than she cared to admit. Her hand reached behind her head and she felt the ivory hair comb he'd surprised her with—for her birthday, he'd clarified when she protested that she hadn't thought to buy him a Christmas present. She'd been unsettled not only by the thoughtfulness of his gift but by how much she liked it.

A rush of heat coursed through her as she remembered the intimacy of Mark's whispered comment as he inserted it into her chignon. *"Frankly, I like it better when you leave your hair loose."*

Of course, he couldn't leave it at that and had immediately issued his usual rebuke of her: *"But I guess that's not the fashion among the social elite."*

"What are you doing here?" Her tone was more challenging than she'd intended, but she couldn't let Mark see how much he unnerved her.

"Senator Overstreet has hired me to find his wife's paintings." Mark's dark eyes pierced her. "And you?"

"Mrs. Hall was here last night and was about to tell me all about it," Marillo said.

"Not yet." Charley turned away from Mark to look at the police detective. "You haven't finished telling me what happened with the two trucks. Where's the second cop?" She shifted her gaze to the officers huddled over the body and then back to Marillo and Mark.

Mark's eyebrows raised. "You haven't told her?" he said to Marillo.

"I haven't gotten to that part yet."

"What part?" Charley's eyes narrowed.

Marillo heaved a sigh. "They weren't cops."

"Not cops? How do you know that?" Charley gaped at Marillo.

"For one thing, police officers don't work as personal security guards for paintings—certainly not in uniform," Marillo said.

"What if a federal senator asks the mayor for a special favour?"

Marillo shook his head.

"It wasn't a very good uniform," Mark added. "Frankly, I'm surprised it fooled anyone."

"Would the average person know that?" Charley thought back to her first encounter with Mark. He'd flashed his detective badge, but she'd never seen a Toronto Police

Department shield before and had wondered at the time if it was real. "So, if he wasn't a cop who was he?"

Marillo shrugged. "Probably another thief."

"Does that mean that the men in the blue truck were the real deal?" she asked. Why would the gallery need armed guards for a bunch of paintings by an unknown artist? It wasn't as if they were dealing with Rembrandts.

"No," Mark said to Charley and turned to Marillo. "That's what I came out to tell you. Overstreet's just received a call from the gallery owner, a Mr. Lee Rosco—"

"Rothko," Charley corrected him. "I met him last evening. Odd little man."

"Ro*th*ko," Mark said, emphasizing the correct pronunciation of the name. "He was calling to say the truck from Toronto is delayed by the storm and won't be able to collect the paintings until the highway's cleared. Probably sometime tomorrow."

"So, we have two sets of thieves?" Charley's mind was whirling.

"Starting to look that way." Marillo cursed under his breath. "What was Rothko's reaction when the senator told him the paintings had been stolen?"

"Judging by the silence on the other end of the line, I'd say he was in shock."

"That seems to be the common reaction," Marillo said. "Mrs. Overstreet is also so overcome she's taken to her bed."

"You haven't spoken with her?" Mark asked.

"Not yet." Marillo sounded defensive. "According to the senator, she was sleeping at the time of the theft. He's asked that we give her some time to recover from the shock."

"Detective!" A young constable approached Marillo. "The examiner is finished with the body and wants to know if it's okay to transport him to the morgue."

"Did he find anything unusual?"

"Nah, nothing except the dead bloke has to be the unluckiest son of a gun in the world. The bullets must have ricocheted off the wall to strike him in the chest."

"That is odd," Mark said.

"Why?" Charley asked.

"It could mean the men in the second van didn't intend to kill, only to scare," Mark said. "And if so, maybe we aren't dealing with vicious criminals who will do anything to get their greedy mitts on the paintings but haphazard lackeys who have gotten themselves in over their heads."

Marillo glared at the two of them. "Enough speculation. This is my case, thank you very much."

Mark held up his hands in mock acquiescence. "Hey, I'm here for the paintings. The murder is all yours."

"That's what she says, too." Marillo didn't look convinced. He turned to the young officer. "Tell the examiner it's okay to take the body. And you fellas, get back to looking for those bullet casings."

"You still haven't found them?" Mark asked.

"There's five inches of snow!" Marillo snapped. "Now, Mrs. Hall, your turn. Tell me about last night."

"Frankly, I don't think I have much to say."

"We had a deal!"

"And I'll keep to it. But you can get the full and accurate guest list from the Overstreets. And I told you I'll send over the photos the *Trib* has from last evening. What you really want to know is whether I saw or heard anything unusual, or if anything out of the ordinary happened while I was there. It didn't. It was a typical, somewhat dull, *vernissage*." In her pocket, Charley surreptitiously crossed her fingers at the lie. The event had been typical but not dull—although not for any reason that would interest the Kingston Police Department.

"All right." Marillo removed his fedora and ran his fingers through his greying hair. "I guess I better go make a statement to the press. What are you going to do?"

"I am going to go see if Mrs. Overstreet would like to give *me* a statement," Charley said.

"You are just going to waltz into the house and ask to speak with her, are you?" Marillo's eyebrows raised in disbelief.

"Yes, Detective Marillo, that is precisely what I'm going to do."

"Oh, Charley—I mean Mrs. Hall. It is lovely to see you. Come in, come in. You, too, Mr. Spadina, if you must."

"Thank you, Mrs. Rinehart. It's lovely to see you, too." Charley stomped her feet on the welcome mat to remove some of the snow before stepping into the familiar foyer. "I missed you last evening at the *vernissage*."

"Oh well, Mrs. Overstreet had everything arranged. I'd have been in the way."

In the way?

That said a lot about the relationship between the long-time housekeeper and the lady of the house. "Between you and me, you didn't miss much," Charley said, unbuttoning her coat. "Unlike all the excitement this morning."

Mrs. Rinehart accepted Charley's and Mark's coats. "I knew there was something fishy about that white truck, right from the start."

"Oh?" Mark paused removing the rubbers from his shoes and glanced up at her. "Why is that?"

"It was the name on the side: 'Toronto Art Gallry'."

"What's so strange about that?" Mark asked.

Mrs. Rinehart arched a perfectly plucked eyebrow at him. That was one of the things Charley always loved about her. She may have been the housekeeper, but she was always impeccably groomed. Her blonde hair (probably dyed now—she was well past the age of fifty, after all) was cut in the latest style, and the smooth texture of her face powder gave her face an unlined, youthful glow. Only her uniform gave away her status. She wore an A-line, navy-blue skirt with a crisp white blouse; a cameo brooch pinned to the high neck was her only adornment. Charley didn't know if there had ever been a Mr. Rinehart; she'd never heard the housekeeper or anyone in the Overstreet family speak of one.

"Gallry," the housekeeper repeated. "G-A-L-L-R-Y. It was missing an 'e'."

"Ah, I see."

"I supposed it could be one of those Toronto eccentricities where they purposely spell words incorrectly, which frankly, I think is abhorrent, but..." She shrugged. "There you have it." She turned to Charley. "Shall I call Poppy for you?"

"No!" Charley didn't mean for her response to be quite so emphatic. "Actually, I am here to see Mrs. Overstreet," she said more sedately.

"I'm not sure that will be possible. She's retired to her room. Quite overwrought. Let me check with the senator." She pointed down at Charley's still booted feet. "In the meantime, you know the drill."

"Yes, ma'am." Charley faked a sharp salute. After the housekeeper walked away, she sat down on the bench and untied her winter boots. She reached into a basket of woollen booties—hand-knitted by Mrs. Rinehart—and slipped a pair on her feet.

"I take it last night wasn't your first visit to this house," Mark said, helping her up.

"I came here a lot when I was a child. I always wished

Mrs. Rinehart would come work for us. I even managed to convince Gran to offer her more money than what the Overstreets could possibly be paying her. She graciously declined."

"She was probably aware of your grandmother's difficulty in keeping domestic staff," Mark chuckled.

"Maybe," she conceded, "but I think it was more a matter of loyalty to the Overstreet family."

She led Mark from the foyer to a large room at the back of the house. "This is the conservatory, where the show was held last evening," she said, crossing to the towering windows that lined the back wall. Outside, a long porch ran the length of the main house. It had a wide, central staircase that led down to what, in the summer, was a manicured carpet of green extending down to Lake Ontario but was now a fluffy blanket of white.

"Many people?" Mark asked.

"Not as many as you'd expect," Charley said. "Many sent their regrets because of the threatening snowstorm. So many, in fact, that Mrs. Overstreet tried to cancel it altogether. But of course, by then it was too late to reach everyone. I would say there were about a dozen of us."

"Anyone of interest?"

Charley gave a non-committal grunt. She'd rather forget last night, but the memory kept returning like a bad penny. Being here again, in this room, was making it impossible to block it out of her mind.

"Didn't we do something similar when we were in the nursery with Nanny?"

Charley turned to the familiar voice. "Dan!" She hadn't seen her childhood friend since his wedding six weeks earlier. She was genuinely pleased to see him, more so because his new bride, Meredith, wasn't standing next to him.

"*What are you doing here?*" As a city alderman, he was required to attend many social functions, but Senator Overstreet's home wasn't in his ward.

"*I am hoping to convince the senator to endorse my nomination to run as a member of Parliament in the next federal election. He hasn't been returning my telephone calls and I thought he might be more receptive if I came here and oozed compliments on his wife's artistic talent.*"

"*In that case, you'd best keep your opinion on Clarice Overstreet's artistic talents to yourself, you philistine.*" The paintings with their aggressive splashes of red and yellow weren't to her liking either.

"*If monochrome is one colour, what do you call something that's only two colours?*"

"*Diochrome?*" Charley chuckled.

"*I don't think diochrome is a real word. C'mon, Charley, you're a writer. You're supposed to know these things.*" His eyes held that familiar twinkle that always made her smile whenever they attended functions together as a couple, as though they were the only two in the room who understood the same joke.

"*It doesn't matter anyway. See where the red and yellow overlap?*" She pointed at the canvas. "*It's orange. So, technically, there are three colours.*" How easily they fell back into their comfortable old banter.

"*Triochrome?*" Dan snickered.

"*Shush, the two of you! I could hear you from across the room.*" Meredith seemed to appear out of nowhere, her eyebrows knitted together and her mouth a firm, hard line. "*It's called Abstract Expressionism, and it's all the rage.*"

"*Sorry, dear.*" Dan gave Meredith a sheepish grin. "*It's simply that I prefer to recognize the subjects in my artwork.*"

"*The whole collection is strikingly powerful,*" Meredith

continued. "Especially when you consider it's been done by a woman. Surely, you understand, Charley."

Charley glanced at the painting on the easel in front of her and then allowed her gaze to roam around the room to the other canvases. All of them were variations of the same painting—broad, seemingly random strokes of red and yellow, some merging into orange, others keeping to the two primary colours.

No, she didn't get it. Meredith's assertion that as a woman she should, made her feel inadequate. She quickly made her excuses and left the event.

"The senator will see you," Mrs. Rinehart said, interrupting Charley's reverie. She led them out of the conservatory and down a short hallway to a walnut-lined study. "Mrs. Hall and Mr. Spadina are here, Senator."

Senator Harold Overstreet rose from where he'd been tending the fire. "Charley, thank you for coming. I simply can't believe it." He drew her into a friendly embrace.

In his mid-fifties, Senator Overstreet was still a remarkably attractive man. He'd retained his full head of hair, now steel-grey, and a trim, athletic physique. Charley always joked that if Dan continued in politics, he'd end up looking like all the other rotund, whiskey-drinking, cigar-chomping politicians they knew. Overstreet was the exception, which was odd given how fond he was of both whiskey and cigars—and women if the rumours were true.

"Spadina." The senator took Mark's hand in his gloved one. "Didn't expect to see you again quite so soon."

"Mrs. Hall and I are old friends, and she has graciously offered to provide some additional intelligence on last evening's event."

"Good, good, good." Overstreet motioned to a pair of

high-back chairs across from his desk. "Have a seat. Can I get you something to drink? Coffee? Tea?"

Charley and Mark both declined.

Overstreet nodded to dismiss Mrs. Rinehart, then rounded the desk and sat down. "Now," he said, leaning back and folding his arms across his chest, "how can I help?"

"I was hoping to speak with Clarice," Charley said. "To round out the article. We'll have to add something about the theft. It can't be helped, I'm afraid."

"Yes, of course, I understand. Unfortunately, Clarice is not up to speaking to anyone right now. As you might imagine, she's absolutely devastated by the loss of her paintings. So much time and effort put in, taken away by a bunch of bold brigands." He stared at Mark. "That's why I hired you. It's not that I don't trust Kingston's police department, but I'm not convinced they'll be able to devote the time and resources needed to solve this thing."

"Given the murder, you mean," Charley said.

"Yes, that." Overstreet's mouth puckered. "Distasteful business, all of it."

"Would you mind telling me what happened after I left last evening? And where everyone was when the theft occurred this morning?"

"I've already gone through this with the police—and Spadina," Overstreet said.

"Yes, but it would be helpful to me and my article if you don't mind." She gave him an encouraging smile.

"Very well." He tapped the gloved fingers of his right hand on the surface of the desk and seemed to consider where to begin. "I don't remember you leaving, but pretty much everyone was gone by nine—the storm, you understand. Poppy went to bed, and Rothko and I helped Clarice crate up her paintings so they could be picked up in the morning."

"What time were they supposed to be collected?"

Overstreet pursed his lips and a line formed between his eyebrows. "No idea. Rothko oversaw all that. But I do know the truck was coming from Toronto."

"I see. Sorry for the interruption. Go on, please."

"Rothko left at ten-thirty. Clarice retired for the evening. I had a brandy in my study and listened to the hourly news on the wireless at eleven, as I always do, and then went up to bed."

"And this morning? Where was everyone when...?"

"When the man was shot?" The senator finished for her. His face had taken on a shiny pink hue. A bead of sweat appeared along his hairline. "Poppy and Clarice were still in bed and I was here, in my office. Mrs. Rinehart was the one who alerted me that there was a commotion outside of the east wing."

"What time was that?"

"Eight-thirty. I went immediately and saw the fellow on the ground. I had her telephone the police once I saw there was nothing I could do for him. He was already dead. And the rest you know." He stood to signal the end of their meeting.

"You didn't hear the gunshots yourself?" Charley asked, rising reluctantly from her chair.

"No, and I wouldn't all the way back here."

Mark stood. "Unless there is anything else you want to add, we best be getting on with our investigation."

"No, nothing else."

"Will you let Clarice know I'd like to speak with her?" Charley asked. "I don't want to upset her, but maybe speaking with another woman would be helpful."

"She's got Poppy, but yes, I will let her know you stopped by and to give you a ring if she feels up to it." Overstreet opened the door to his study. "You remember your way out, I assume, Charley?"

"Yes, of course. We'll make our own way. No need to disturb Mrs. Rinehart." She followed Mark out the door but paused on the threshold. "Are you feeling all right, Senator?"

"Yes, of course. Why do you ask?"

"You've not taken off your gloves after you tended the fire."

Overstreet looked down at his hands. "I love this old house, but alas, it's very drafty."

Charley had found the room uncomfortably warm, but she didn't press him. She knew that as people age, their perception of temperature could change. Gran often complained about the heat or cold when Charley found a room quite comfortable. But she was in her eighties.

Charley trailed Mark to the foyer. "So, what's next?"

"What I'd really like is to see Mrs. Overstreet's art studio. The police were in and out—Marillo said there was nothing there—but now it's locked up tight. The senator says it's because his wife doesn't allow anyone in her studio, not even the housekeeper. So, until we can speak to her..." He left the rest of the sentence hanging.

"What do you think you'll find in the studio?"

"I don't know. I'm trying to figure out why someone would want to steal a collection of paintings done by a woman who hasn't even had her first formal art show. What's so special about them? Or was it something else they were after?"

"Follow me." Charley made an abrupt turn and led Mark toward the east wing.

"Hey, hold up, Tiger." Mark grabbed her arm. "Don't you think I already tried to get in?"

"Oh, ye of little faith." Charley wrenched her arm away and continued to the wing's entrance. She tried to turn the doorknob, but it wouldn't budge.

"See? I told you so."

She cocked an eyebrow at his smugness. Mark Spadina had a habit of getting the better of her, but not this time. She stood on her toes and reached up to the top of the door jamb.

Please, be here.

She ran her fingertips along the smooth surface, her heart racing. It would be so embarrassing to be wrong.

No, wait. There it is!

She plucked the key from its resting place and slid it into the lock, swinging the door open with a flourish. "You were saying?"

"I'm impressed," Mark said, following her into the room. "What other Overstreets secrets do you know?"

"You'll have to wait and see."

The entire wing appeared to be one huge room, brightly lit from the large windows along the front and back exterior walls. It was a perfect art studio, just as it had been a perfect rumpus room when she'd played here in her youth. Gone were the shelves of games and books, and the grand dollhouse she'd envied. In their place was...nothing. No easels, no canvases, no paint, no brushes. The only telltale sign that anyone had been in here recently was the melted slush from the boots of whoever had taken the paintings and the police officers who'd come to investigate the theft.

"I'm guessing that despite the senator's claim that no one is allowed in the wing, the housekeeper comes in to clean. That's how you knew where the key was?" Mark said, scanning the room.

"Maybe. But when I was last here, the room was considered off-limits, too—it was supposed to be for the children, no adults allowed. Mrs. Rinehart kept a key hidden, of course, so she could check on the room, but it was up to us to keep it neat and tidy." Charley swung her arm around dramatically. "But this?" She couldn't imagine, given the aggressive, almost violent application of paint she'd seen in the artwork last evening that there'd be no trace of it in the studio. The woman who'd created those paintings didn't seem to be the sort who would be fanatical about keeping her art studio pristine. "Even if Mrs. Rinehart was coming in to tidy, why is there no splash of paint anywhere?"

"There's not much of anything," Mark agreed. "But you know how temperamental these creative types can be. Maybe she was taking a break or suffering from whatever the painter's equivalent is for writer's block," Mark said, coming to stand beside her. "Speaking of temperamental creatives, do you want to let me in on your history with the Overstreet family?"

"Not really."

Mark crossed his arms and pierced her with one of his penetrating stares.

"It was a long time ago. Until last night, I hadn't been here in years." She squirmed under his scrutiny. "Besides, it has nothing to do with the case."

"Hmm. There didn't seem to be any tension between you and the senator," Mark mused. "And Mrs. Rinehart seemed genuinely pleased to see you. Mrs. Overstreet?"

"You're fishing, Detective. And wasting our time."

"Finding more out about you is never a waste of my

time, Tiger," Mark teased. "Let's see, now, if it's not Mrs. Over—"

"Well, well, well, look who the cat dragged in!"

Charley stiffened. *Great!* Slowly, she turned around to face the inevitable.

Mark stepped past her. "You must be Poppy. We were just talking about you."

CHARLEY HAD SUCCESSFULLY MANAGED to avoid Poppy last evening, but this morning her luck had run out.

"Poppy, this is Private Detective Mark Spadina. Your father hired him to find the stolen paintings. Mark, this is Poppy Tremblay, Senator Overstreet's daughter."

"That explains what you're doing in step-mama's private sanctuary." Poppy took Mark's offered hand and held it a tad longer than necessary. "I've never met a real private detective before. How exciting."

"Step-mama?" Mark asked.

"Yes. Did Daddy forget to mention that?"

"Poppy lives in Montreal with her husband and what is it? Three children now?" Charley asked.

"Two." Poppy glared at her.

"I'm surprised they're not here. Roland, too."

"It was a very last-minute thing. I didn't want to take the children out of school, and Roland is terribly busy."

"Investment banker," Charley said for Mark's benefit.

"Interesting," Mark said.

"Not really, but it keeps him busy and out of my way." Poppy glanced around the room. "It's been ages since I've been in here. I hate how chopped up it's become."

"Chopped up?" Charley repeated.

"Surely, you can tell. She's blocked off a big chunk at the end for her *studio*. Apparently, this whole room was too overwhelming."

"Huh." Now that Poppy mentioned it, the room did seem smaller than Charley remembered. She should have caught the discrepancy sooner. But it had been years and she'd been smaller, too.

The exterior door of the wing should have been in the centre of the north wall, but it now appeared to be two-thirds down. She walked to the end of the room and tried the handle to what she had assumed was a storage closet.

"Yes, through that door is her private kingdom into which none of us mere mortals are allowed," Poppy sneered.

"No one?" Charley stood on her toes and ran her finger along the top of the door jamb, but this time there was no key.

"Not even Mrs. Rinehart." Poppy turned to Mark and slipped her arm through his. "Since you are going to be working for us, shall I give you the full tour? I can answer any questions you have at the same time."

Charley rolled her eyes. Poppy would never change. She'd always been a flirt. "We're pretty much done here."

"Actually, I do have some questions for you, Mrs. Tremblay," Mark said, turning them away from Charley's scowl.

"Poppy, please." She smiled coyly.

"Poppy, then." He turned back and winked at Charley.

Charley wanted to wipe that goofy grin from Mark's face. What did men see in Poppy? She tried to look at her childhood friend without the bias she'd amassed over those years of resentment. Long, flowing blonde curls that never fell out of place, soft ivory skin, and a body with the curves of a pin-up girl. Not too tall. Not too short. Charley raised her hand to try to order her own messy mass of chestnut-coloured curls. She felt the comb Mark had given her and jabbed it tighter against her head. The top of Poppy's head came up to Mark's shoulder, while Charley could almost look him in the eye.

"How long has your father been married to your step-mother?" Mark asked.

"It's been a little over a year." She paused and then added with a note of disdain, "Mother died May of '47 and Daddy wed Clarice in November that same year."

"I heard you introduced them," Charley said, stirring the pot. What she'd heard through the grapevine was that Poppy had inadvertently brought them together and was furious with the union.

"Not quite," Poppy huffed. "Daddy came to stay with us after Mother died and he met her at a *café* around the corner, where he'd go for his paper and morning coffee. She was a waitress."

"Sounds romantic. Like a Hollywood movie," Charley said, enjoying Poppy's discomfort. "Your father is still quite dashing. He must have swept her off her feet. She's quite young, isn't she?"

"Twenty-six."

Charley resisted the urge to point out that Clarice was three years younger than Poppy—and herself for that matter.

Mark glanced between the two women, his brow furrowed as if he was trying to figure out what was going on. The undercurrent of hostility was unmistakable. "The two of you seem to know a lot about each other."

"We used to be the best of friends, didn't we Charley?" Poppy's smile was a saccharine imitation of affection.

"When we were very young."

"What happened?" Mark asked.

"Oh, you know the old story. A boy." Poppy's eyes narrowed as she turned to Charley. "I talked to Dan last night and we regaled his *bride* with stories of our misadventures. She's charming, isn't she? I think they'll be *very* happy."

And there it was. Her teenage angst laid bare. Charley had confided her feelings for Dan to her best girlfriend, and Poppy had gone right out and set her cap for him anyway.

"Yes, the wedding was lovely, wasn't it, Mark?" Charley said, trying to salvage as much of her pride as she could. "I didn't see you there, Poppy, even though I'd heard you were home for the holidays."

"Christmas is such a busy time of the year," Poppy said dismissively. She turned her head to look up at Mark. "Now, I'm afraid I must leave you to attend to some personal matters. But do telephone me, Detective, if there's anything, anything at all, that I can do for you." She patted his arm and then sashayed out of the room, totally ignoring Charley, and swaying her hips in a way that indicated she was fully aware that Mark's gaze was following her.

"Well, that was enlightening," Mark said, turning back to face Charley.

"Don't read too much into anything she says."

"No ma'am." Mark grinned. "But I'm getting to know you a whole lot better."

"Can we get back to the case?"

"Sure." Mark's expression sobered. "I'm still at a loss as to what's so important about these paintings. I need to talk to the gallery owner, but I'd feel better if I had some more background on that type of art first."

Charley hesitated. She knew the perfect person for them to talk to, but she was reluctant to suggest her after last night's chastisement. Then again, she didn't need to go with

Mark, did she? He was the one who had to solve the crime. She already had enough information to finish her article. However, being able to write a first-person account of how they found the thieves and recovered the artwork would be a huge scoop for both her and the *Trib*.

Mark was looking at her expectantly. For once, he seemed willing to include her in his investigation. She took a deep breath.

Really, how bad could it be?

"I know someone who can help us."

CHARLEY TIGHTENED the scarf around her neck and gazed out from beneath the carriage porch. Aside from the two police constables who were on their knees in the driveway sifting through the accumulating mound of snow for bullet shell casings, everyone—including Lester—had gone. She wondered what he'd write for his article. How much had Marillo told the reporters about the dead "cop"?

She pushed aside her curiosity. It wasn't her story.

Too bad.

She turned to Mark. "Maybe we should talk to Meredith via telephone. The roads are pretty much impassable by automobile."

"I thought we'd walk."

"Walk?" She eyed him sharply, not relishing the idea of a three-mile trudge through ankle-deep snow to the Bankses' mansion on Front Road. "Don't you think it's a little far?"

"I thought you went everywhere on foot." Mark's eyes narrowed. "Or are you a fair-weather walker?"

"Fine." She smashed her hat on her head and stepped out from the protection of the carriage porch. At least Mark was less likely to complain the whole way as Lester had.

At the bottom of the driveway, she turned to go west on King Street, but Mark stopped her. "Where are you going?"

"To the Bankses', of course." She pulled her arm free.

Mark shook his head and tsked. "Cannon didn't tell you?"

"Tell me what?" She hated when he dangled bits and pieces of information that he insinuated she should already know.

"The newlyweds recently moved into a *modest* six-bedroom starter home a few blocks from here. I guess if Cannon is going to run in the next federal election, he needs to live in the riding. The Bankses' place is too far out." Mark's gaze was pitying. "I can't believe you didn't know that."

"I haven't spoken to either of them since their wedding on Christmas Eve," Charley said, crossing her fingers inside her mitten. *Except for last night.* But neither Dan nor Meredith had bothered to mention their new home then. "How did you find out?"

"Rose. Who else?" Mark said.

"Look at you, all part of the family," she said, irritated that Dan's mother hadn't said anything to her about the move, either. Did Gran know?

"It's this way." Mark took her elbow and led her across the street.

She knew she shouldn't be upset with Mark. He was Dan's half-brother, so technically he *was* part of the family. But up until now, he'd seemed to go out of his way to avoid any familial attachments to the Cannons. Had something happened in the past few months to change that?

Well, why not? A lot had changed for Charley since she'd last seen the private detective.

Up until a few months ago, she and Dan had been the

best of friends. Neither would have considered making any sort of major decision without talking with the other first. But with his engagement to Meredith Banks, and now his purchase of a new home, she'd been kept totally in the dark.

She was guilty, too. She hadn't told him about the bombshell Freddie had dropped on her at Christmas. Her brother had confirmed that Theo, her husband, listed as missing since 1942, was dead—he'd died in Freddie's arms as they'd come ashore on the beach at Dieppe, in France.

She'd barely returned from Dan's wedding when Freddie had finally told her. The irony of that! It was the prospect that Theo could still be alive, could still come home even after six years, that had stopped her from accepting Dan's many marriage proposals. At least that was what she'd told him—and herself.

She couldn't explain why she'd kept Freddie's disclosure to herself. It wasn't as if she thought she was doing Meredith a favour—that if Dan knew the truth he would leave his wife for Charley.

Or was it?

When he'd first gotten engaged, Dan had told Charley he'd end it if she would agree to marry him. But they'd both known it was impossible at the time. Theo was still missing. There was still a chance that the husband she loved—even if she wasn't *in love* with him—could return home. She'd promised she'd be there waiting for him when he did.

She hadn't mentioned Freddie's revelation to Mark, either, telling herself she wanted to avoid his "I told you so." But she wasn't sure that was all of it.

Mark was an enigma. He revealed little about himself and what he did share, she couldn't be certain was entirely truthful. But he had a keen knack for seeing beneath the mask she put on for the world. If he knew the truth, he'd confront her about her feelings for both Theo and Dan, and how she'd used one to keep the other at arm's length for years—choosing to live a life in limbo because deep down she knew she didn't love Dan enough to give up her independence for him.

Freddie's reason for finally telling her about Theo had had little to do with providing her with peace of mind and more to do with supporting his own sobriety. He'd suggested she already knew—had to have known—at least deep down. There may have been something to that, but it didn't mean the person she thought she was and the life she'd built wasn't upended by his confirmation of it.

"Here we are," Mark said.

The home they'd arrived at was of a stately Victorian design, possessing an orange brick *façade* and a mansard roof with a square, flat-topped tower. An elegant, white, covered entrance jutted out from the front and extended upward to a second-storey balcony. Yes, even by her privileged standards, she'd be hard pressed to call Dan's new home "modest." She followed Mark up the wide front steps and waited while he rapped on the door.

Charley recognized the woman who answered as the housekeeper from the Bankses' mansion. She must have relocated with Meredith.

"Hello, Mrs. Harper," Mark said. "We'd like to speak with Mrs. Cannon if she's available."

Mrs. Cannon? She immediately imagined Dan's mother, but of course, Rose was no longer the sole Mrs. Cannon in the family. Still, Mark's use of the name caught Charley by surprise.

"Of course. Come in, Detective. It's a pleasure to see you again, too, Mrs. Hall." She took their damp coats and waited while Charley removed her boots—no cozy slippers to put on here. She indicated they were to wait in a sitting room at the front of the house and went to retrieve Meredith.

Charley walked to the fireplace and rubbed her chilled fingertips while she took in the room. It was classically decorated: an expansive hardwood floor scattered with woven rugs, wainscoting circling the room, and furniture that was neither overly large nor overly bright. A few formal family photographs were properly positioned on various tables. On the walls were three paintings that were so inoffensive as to be banal. No one would find fault with the room—and that was certainly the intention—but its total lack of personality grated on Charley. The room was a reflection of Meredith: faultless but innocuous. There was no trace of Dan's vibrant personality anywhere.

"Charley. Mark. How lovely." Meredith glided into the room wearing an indigo-coloured dress with a low-slung sarong skirt and form-fitting, vee-neck bodice that had long sleeves and padded shoulders. Her pale blonde hair was pulled back into a low bun, a plaited braid wrapped around the base completing the elegant style.

Charley fought against making comparisons with her own comfortable high-waisted trousers and silk shirt cut in a simple style. She was working, after all. Her clothing had to be practical. She gave Meredith and her perfectly made-up face another glance. As the wife of a future politician, she was dressed for work, too, although how she could have ever anticipated visitors during a major snowstorm baffled Charley.

"Hello, Angel," Mark greeted Meredith. "Sorry to barge in on you unannounced."

Meredith turned up her cheek for Mark to kiss it, confirming Charley's suspicion that he'd become closer to the family than he was prepared to admit. As the woman turned to her, Charley feared she'd be expecting a similar affectionate greeting, so she quickly extended her hand as a more formal gesture.

"I'm sorry Dan can't join us. He insisted on going to the shipyard. Imagine, in this frightful weather! But it's lovely to see the two of you. May I offer you something to help warm you up?" Meredith picked up a silver bell from a side table and jingled it. A young woman came in to take their requests, and they all decided apple cider would be "most agreeable" on this cold, snowy day.

"We're not here on a social call," Charley said once they'd settled with their ciders.

"I didn't think so," Meredith said, winking at Mark. "When the two of you get together, it usually means someone's been murdered."

"Not this time," Mark said.

"Actually, there was a murder earlier this morning, "Charley corrected him. "But that's not why we're here, although it is related."

Meredith sat forward, her pale blue eyes wide. "And you think I can help in some way? How intriguing."

"The *Rouge et Jaune* collection was stolen earlier this morning," Charley said. "Mark has been hired by Senator Overstreet to recover it."

"Oh dear, that's awful." Meredith's hand flew to her mouth. "Poor Clarice. She must be a wreck."

"I tried to see her, but the senator says she's too distraught to talk to anyone. Even the police."

"I don't doubt it. The passion and power in those paintings... She poured her poor, broken heart into them. It must feel as if she's been personally violated."

"Broken heart?" Charley asked.

Meredith looked down. Even the pinking of her cheeks was elegantly accomplished. "I shouldn't have said anything. The last thing I want is to be known as a gossip."

"It's not gossip. It may be relevant to our investigation." Charley turned to Mark, her eyes imploring him to intervene.

"Charley's got a point," Mark said. "We're at the beginning of our inquiry. Any bit of information could be relevant."

"I promise, we won't share anything you tell us with anyone unless it proves to be important to the case," Charley said. "And even then, we won't say where it came from."

"I suppose it's not a secret. Both Dan and my brother have commented on it," Meredith said, although she still looked troubled.

"Dan and Colin have discussed Clarice's broken heart?" Charley asked.

"No, not directly." Meredith took a sip of her cider and seemed to be considering whether she should elaborate. She put her mug down on the coffee table and squared her shoulders. "In addition to being wealthy and very influential, Senator Overstreet is an extremely attractive man," she began.

Charley tried to imagine him as other women might. "For his age, I guess," she conceded, unable to think of him as anything other than a father figure.

"I understand his first marriage wasn't a very happy union," Meredith said.

"I can attest to that," Charley said. "It was arranged by their parents, but it didn't seem to suit either of them. They lived separate lives. Everyone knew that."

"Yes, well, apparently his separate life included many

mistresses in Ottawa, where he spent most of his time on Senate business," Meredith said. "After his first wife died, he married Clarice but evidently he has *not* changed his ways."

"You mean he still has mistresses in Ottawa?" Charley asked.

"He spends all week there, leaving poor Clarice here all by herself."

"His job is in Ottawa." Charley hadn't liked the first Mrs. Overstreet and knew little about the second, but she'd always been fond of the senator and didn't want to think ill of him. It was one thing to have mistresses during an unhappy marriage, but presumably he'd learned his lesson and his marriage to Clarice had been a love match. A young waitress certainly couldn't have brought anything else to their union.

"But his wife stays in Kingston," Meredith said.

"And you think her paintings are an expression of her misery?" Mark asked.

"And her anger, and her disappointment. All of it. You saw them, Charley. Do they seem the work of a happy young bride?"

"Frankly, I couldn't make heads nor tails out of them," Charley admitted. "They didn't appeal to me at all."

"Abstract Expressionism isn't for everyone," Meredith agreed.

"Why would someone want to steal the paintings of an unknown artist?" Mark asked.

"Well, for one thing, the paintings were very good," Meredith said. "But you're right, Clarice hadn't even had her first exhibition. It did strike me as a bit odd, though, that the gallery she chose was in Toronto, not Montreal."

"Because she's from Montreal?" Charley asked.

"No, not that. Although now you mention it, that is funny, isn't it? You'd think she'd like to show off to her hometown. No, I was thinking it's strange because Montreal is very forward-thinking and adventuresome with regard to art and culture. From what I've read, Toronto is more conservative."

"I think that's a fair assessment," Mark agreed. He'd grown up in Toronto and had been a police detective there before a murder brought him to Kingston. "I'm not familiar with this type of art you're talking about. Can you explain more?"

"I'm hardly an expert but I have read some articles about it."

"It comes from Europe?" Charley asked. Meredith had gone to boarding school in Switzerland.

"New York City," Meredith said. "There are two broad groups within the movement: action painters who attack their canvas with expressive brush strokes, and colour field painters who fill their canvases with large areas of a single colour. Clarice's paintings seemed to bridge the two. Oh!" Meredith sat up straighter. "Perhaps that's it. Maybe she is the bridge."

"Bridge?" Mark asked.

"Oh yes, the entity that brings unity to the movement," she said excitedly. "Imagine, Charley, we saw her works before anyone else."

"And you think this 'bridge' would be a motive for the collection to be stolen?" Mark asked.

"Of course. Either way."

"Either way?" Charley repeated.

"Either by someone who wants to have a piece of this moment in history when the two branches are united or by someone who wants to stop it from happening."

"If Clarice can't show her collection, no one will know they are this bridge you talk about," Charley said. "So, what is their value to a thief in your first scenario? Who would buy them?"

"What you must realize, Charley, is that most art collectors want the works for their own pleasure, not to resell them. Much of the art that's been stolen over the centuries is probably hanging on the walls of private homes."

"But if it's the second scenario—someone wants to make sure there is no unity between the two branches—what's to stop Clarice from simply doing more paintings?" Mark asked.

"Ah, so practical, Detective Spadina," Meredith scoffed gently. "If you had seen the collection, you'd understand how emotionally wrought she must be to have it taken from her—like losing a limb...no, a child. When a child is lost, you can't simply replace it with another, can you? I fear Clarice may never pick up a paintbrush again. And if she does, is she likely to replicate what she's lost? I don't think so. She has been changed by the experience. It will be reflected in her art going forward." Meredith frowned.

"Another possibility is it's both scenarios. There were two sets of thieves," Charley said.

"Two?" Meredith was incredulous.

"It seems Mrs. Overstreet's collection is very popular among the criminal element," Mark said dryly.

"You know, you should talk to Jean-Philippe Leloup," Meredith said.

"Who is he?" Mark asked.

"An art critic." She glanced at Charley. "He was there last night."

"I didn't see him," Charley said.

"Maybe not. He came late. Not a very pleasant man, I

have to say. He took over the room as soon as he arrived and dominated Clarice's time for the rest of the evening. We couldn't even offer her a proper goodbye when we left. I gather he contributes to various influential art publications, so I don't suppose we can blame her for giving him all her attention."

"Do you know if he's still in town?" Mark asked.

"Look outside. I don't think anyone is going anywhere until this snowstorm stops."

"Does it help? Knowing you were one of the chaps who liberated Holland?"

Freddie's question, coming from the dining room, made Charley stop in her tracks. She stepped to the side of the door jamb so she couldn't be seen and waited for Mark's answer. He rarely talked about any part of his life, but he was exceptionally closed-mouthed about his experiences during World War II.

"Sometimes," Mark replied. "But other times, even that memory can't lift the dark cloud that comes when I think about all the rest of it."

"Italy?" Freddie asked. "Some of the fellows in my sobriety group have told stories. Frankly, when I hear them, I'm torn between relief that I was locked up away from the action and wishing I'd been there to fight with my brothers."

"I don't imagine Jerry's POW camps were a cakewalk, but trust me, Italy was its own special hell."

"Charlotte!" The nasally accented voice behind made her jump. "Are you going to stand there all day or are you going in?"

Charley turned quickly to face her maternal grandmother. "Hello, Evelyn. I was trying to remember if I'd tied up all the loose ends in the article I filed with the *Trib*," she said, crossing her fingers behind her back, but ridiculously pleased with how quickly the fib had come to her. It sounded plausible.

She'd telephoned Grace Fletcher, the *Tribune's* archivist, and top researcher, from Meredith's home to ask her to track down where Jean-Philippe Leloup was staying. While they waited for her to get back to them, Charley and Mark returned to her home so she could finish writing her article and then telephone Grace again to dictate it to her in time to make the deadline for the newspaper's afternoon edition. She hadn't seen Brownie's photographs of the event, but she trusted Grace to pick one or two to accompany her story. And she'd asked for two full sets of last night's photos to be delivered to her home—one for her and Mark, and the other for Detective Marillo and the Kingston Police Department.

She'd left Mark in the drawing room, but he seemed to have migrated to the dining room. No surprise there. The man must have a hollow leg given how often he complained about being hungry. As she followed Evelyn into the dining room, she noted three empty plates in front of Mark. In contrast, her brother had a cup of tea.

Both men leapt to their feet.

"Grandmama." Freddie rounded the table and kissed Evelyn's cheek. "May I introduce Mister Mark Spadina, a private detective friend of Charley's. Mark, this is Lady Evelyn Pierrepont, Countess of Thorton and our grand-mother visiting from England."

"I've already had the pleasure," Mark said, bowing his head respectfully. "It's nice to see you again, Lady Thorton."

"Evelyn, please," she said to Charley's amazement. Had her aristocratic grandmother been slumming in the colonies for so long she'd adopted their more casual form of address? Or maybe it was Mark, himself. Gran, too, permitted him to call her "Bessie", a rarity for all but her closest friends.

"It would be my honour, Evelyn," Mark replied.

Charley's eyes narrowed as she scrutinized the private detective. Black hair. Black eyes. Crooked nose. He was broad and imposing, but in a way that felt more threatening than protective. Maybe it was his rough edges that appealed to older, more refined women. Or maybe it was all that crime fiction Bessie, and now Evelyn, had been reading lately for book club. She'd have to explain to them that the stories of Agatha Christie, Raymond Chandler, and others romanticized both the grisly murders they depicted as well as the detectives who solved them.

"If you will all excuse me, I need to finish reading Mr. Mitchell's *Who Has Seen the Wind,*" Freddie said. "I'm to lead a group discussion on how its themes relate to the nineteenth-century poem of the same name."

"Thanks for keeping me company, Professor," Mark said.

"Oh dear, I was hoping we could all have tea together," Evelyn said. "Oh, well, how about you two? Shall we retire to the drawing room?"

As if on cue, the housekeeper arrived to clear away Mark's dishes. "Would you like anything else, Detective?"

"I think we're all going to have tea in the drawing room, Rachel," Mark said.

With her back to Evelyn, Charley gave him a scowl. She'd prefer to spend as little time as possible with the woman who had made no secret of the fact she was here solely to convince Freddie, heir to the Thorton Earldom, to return to England with her in the spring.

"Why the sour puss?" Mark whispered as they followed Evelyn to the drawing room. "We've got nothing else to do but wait for Grace to call us with Leloup's whereabouts. Have you had anything to eat? Maybe that's why you're in a mood."

"I am not in a mood," Charley hissed back. "I simply don't want to have tea alone with her." Why did Gran pick today, of all days, to volunteer at the local public library? Who was going to be there in this weather, anyway?

"You're not alone, Tiger. I'm here." He gave her a dazzling smile that did nothing to soothe her irritation.

What is taking Grace so long?

"I didn't see your article about the art exhibit in the early edition," Evelyn said once they'd settled into their seats.

"You were looking for it?" Charley was surprised.

"Of course, I read everything you write, but I was especially anxious to read this one. I am always interested in the newer art forms."

"Are you familiar with Abstract Expressionism?" Mark asked.

"No, not at all. I am quite a fan of Surrealism, though." She cocked her head to the side and looked coy. "I met Pablo Picasso, you know."

"Did you?" Mark leaned forward. "He was once suspected of stealing the Mona Lisa, wasn't he?"

"Oh yes, but he wasn't guilty of that. On the other hand, he most certainly was involved in the theft of some Iberian statue heads that were taken from the Louvre, in 1907."

"So, he was an art thief?" Charley's reporter instincts went on high alert. This could be a fascinating addition to her story about recovering Clarice Overstreet's paintings—if they did.

"They were found in his dresser," Evelyn said as if that resolved the whole problem of the theft. "But more important is how the statue heads influenced Pablo's art."

"How so?" Charley was fascinated.

"Are you familiar with his painting *Les Demoiselles d'Avignon*? It's believed that some of the faces of the five naked women it portrays are inspired by the stolen statue heads."

"Why is that significant?"

"It changed everything, didn't it? He abandoned traditional art and re-imagined the human body as a series of geometric shapes. And the rest, as they say, is Surrealism." She chuckled at her play on the familiar phrase.

"You say you met him. What was he like?" Charley glanced back over her shoulder at the side table. She knew there was a pad of paper and a pencil in the left-hand drawer. Would Evelyn be offended if she got them and started taking notes of their conversation?

"He was an artist." Evelyn waved her hand dramatically. "He once brought his mistress to a party that was being hosted by a proper French aristocrat. Everyone was horrified."

"But not you?" Mark asked.

"Of course, I was," Evelyn replied in mock indignation. She leaned forward with a sly smile. "That was half the fun."

Charley couldn't resist any longer. As she rose to get the paper and pencil, Rachel arrived with the tea tray. After placing it on the side table, the housekeeper handed Charley a slip of paper. "From Miss Fletcher," she said.

Charley glanced down at the name of the hotel she'd written.

"I'm sorry Evelyn, but we've got to go," she said, making sure to grab a cookie off the tray. She hadn't eaten lunch and Mark may have had a point about her mood.

CHARLEY AND MARK found Jean-Philippe Leloup in the downtown bar where the hotel manager said he'd be. It looked like he'd been there quite a while.

Leloup eyed them suspiciously as they sat down at his table. "Whatever you're selling, I'm not interested," he said and then downed the amber contents of his glass. "Another!" he roared at the bartender, holding up his empty glass. "Less water this time."

"Put it on my tab," Mark called out. "And a couple of whiskeys, easy on the water." He smiled at Leloup. "You've got to keep on top of these guys, otherwise you'll be drinking nothing but clear, blue Lake Ontario, right?"

The bar was busier than Charley would have expected for the middle of a Friday afternoon, but then, what else was there to do? Most businesses had either not bothered to open or had closed early due to the storm. A group of four men was huddled over a pool table in the corner, and another pair was shooting darts in the back. Most of the bar stools were occupied, too. She was the only woman in the place.

The bartender set a glass down in front of each of them and then unceremoniously thumped a beer mug full of water down on the table. "Add your own damn water."

Both Mark and Leloup lifted their glasses to their lips to drink the alcohol straight. Given its pale colour, Charley guessed it was probably already liberally doused with water but picked up the mug and added more to her glass anyway. She hadn't eaten much today, and she wanted to keep her wits about her. She'd leave it to Mark to build rapport by matching their suspect drink for drink.

It had been easy to spot Jean-Philippe Leloup. His shoulder-length grey hair, triangularly trimmed goatee, and flamboyant purple scarf set him apart from the rest of the bar's clientele.

"All right," he said, swallowing the contents of his glass. "What do you want?" He had a trace of a French accent.

"Only to talk," Mark said, raising his arm to catch the attention of the bartender and indicating he wanted another round. "Mrs. Hall, here, is a reporter. She's writing a story about Clarice Overstreet's art exhibit. We understand you were at the *vernissage* last evening."

"I was sorry to miss you, Monsieur Leloup," Charley said. "If I'd known you were coming, I wouldn't have left so early."

"I don't talk to reporters," Leloup said.

"Oh, dear." Charley sniffed and blinked her eyes rapidly as if trying to stave off tears. "My editor will be so terribly upset if I don't produce a story, but I know so little about art. I was hoping...well, I don't want to impose, but..." She accepted the handkerchief Mark handed her and dabbed her eyes.

Leloup's eyes widened in alarm.

"Mrs. Hall's husband perished in the war and she needs this job to make ends meet. You understand, I'm sure," Mark inserted smoothly.

"I don't even have to mention your name...although it

would add ever so much credibility to my article," Charley implored.

"Well, I don't suppose it would hurt." Leloup glanced between Charley and Mark. "What do you want to know, Mrs. Hall?"

"Wonderful. I can't thank you enough, Monsieur." Charley beamed at him. She reached into her pocketbook and took out her notepad and pencil. "What was your impression of Mrs. Overstreet's collection?"

"*Ça pue!* Absolute garbage."

"But you came all the way from Montreal to see it," Charley said.

"And what a waste of my time it has been. And now, to add insult to injury, I am stuck here waiting for the roads to clear so my bus can take me back."

"What was your purpose in coming?" Mark asked.

"I contribute to a number of publications on the arts. As *chroniqueur*, not a reporter like you, Mrs. Hall."

Charley would have dearly loved to confront him on the differences but kept quiet. He was talking to her because he saw her as a damsel in distress and would close up like a clam if he knew the real reason they wanted to interview him. "And what will *you* write about the collection?" she said instead.

"I don't intend to write anything at all. I was brought here under false pretenses. Mrs. Overstreet's paintings are amateurish. Poor imitations of *Les Automatistes*."

"What is *Les Automatistes*?" she asked.

"You know nothing about art, do you, Mrs. Hall?"

Charley bit the inside of her cheek. She didn't know if Leloup's obnoxiousness was due to the alcohol or his true nature. She suspected it was the latter. She smiled sweetly. "Which is why I've come to you, Monsieur."

"*Les Automatistes* is a movement of *Québéc* artists who are influenced by the joint forces of Surrealism and Automatism."

"Surrealism, like Picasso?" Mark asked.

Leloup rolled his eyes. "Always Picasso with you *Anglais*." He turned to Charley. "Surrealist Automatism is a method of creation in which the artist surrenders conscious control over the process."

"And you think Mrs. Overstreet was trying to imitate this?" she asked.

"Poorly."

"How can you tell?"

"The brush strokes were deliberate. And the colours...?" He shrugged. "Crude."

"If her paintings were so awful, why would Mr. Rothko want to display them in his gallery?" Charley asked.

"I am quite convinced Senator Overstreet is paying Monsieur Rothko to exhibit them. And of course, it is a gallery in Toronto, a city where the Group of Seven is considered *avant-garde*. No reputable gallery owner would dare mount a show of such inferior quality in *Montréal*." He flung his hand in a dismissive gesture and ended up knocking his glass to the floor, where it shattered. "*Merde!*"

Mark stood. "I'll get you another and I'll settle our bill. Do you have enough for your article, Mrs. Hall?"

Charley nodded and rose, too. "Yes. Thank you, Monsieur Leloup. I hope the storm ends soon so you can catch your bus home."

Mark returned with a fresh whiskey. "I don't know if you've heard," he said, holding onto the glass, "but Mrs. Overstreet's entire collection was stolen earlier this morning."

"She should be happy someone has spared her the

embarrassment of exhibiting it." Leloup held out his hand for the drink but Mark kept it just out of reach.

"Given how awful her paintings were, do you know why someone would want to steal them?" Mark asked.

"If we're lucky, to burn them. They are an assault to the eye."

Mark placed the glass on the table, thanked Leloup for his time, and took Charley's elbow to escort her out of the bar.

"What an arrogant man," Charley said.

"Are her paintings that bad?" Mark asked.

"How would I know? They're not to my taste, but Meredith thought they were brilliant."

"Maybe he doesn't like female artists," Mark suggested.

"Female artists, female reporters." She shivered from repulsion, not the chilly air.

"You play the ditzy broad very well, Tiger. I wasn't sure you had it in you."

"It comes in handy, especially when you're dealing with a pretentious nitwit."

"I guess I should be pleased that you've not had to employ that tactic with me."

"Are you so sure I haven't?" Charley asked and was rewarded by the look of confusion that creased his forehead. It was rare that she got the upper hand with him. "Are we going to see Lee Rothko now?"

"No. I called him while you were filing your article and he asked me to postpone our meeting until tomorrow. It's just as well. It's getting late. I'll walk you home."

"Don't bother," Charley said. "It's the wrong direction for you. And I wouldn't mind the time to gather my thoughts about the case."

"As you wish." Mark began to walk away.

"Can I ask you something, first?"

He turned back.

"At the house, earlier, you called Freddie 'Professor'." Mark had a nickname for almost everyone. Grace was "Doll", Meredith was "Angel", and Dan was "Sport".

"So?"

"I thought he was 'Cap'n'."

Mark cocked his head. "He didn't like it. Asked me to call him something else."

"If I asked you to stop calling me 'Tiger,' would you?"

"No." Mark turned and walked away.

Silly question. She didn't know why she even bothered to ask.

Charley didn't recognize the young officer behind the reception desk in the lobby of the police headquarters the next morning. She'd heard the city had hired several new men to accommodate the expanding population in Kingston as young men flocked to the city looking for work, married and started families. And, of course, they'd had to replace Constable Adams, who'd been killed shortly before Christmas. The memory of his death still distressed her.

"I'm here to see Detective Marillo," she said.

"Is he expecting you?" the man asked, not looking up from whatever he was reading. He'd given her a cursory glance when she entered the building, but obviously deemed her unworthy of his attention.

"He most certainly is," Marillo said stepping out from the Sergeant's office, which was off to the right of the main door. "And put away that magazine, Constable. I don't care if you're unhappy about pulling the weekend shift. Your job is to greet visitors and make sure things run smoothly. See that you do it, or I'll have something to report to Sergeant Kearn Monday morning."

"Yes sir!" The young constable flushed at the reprimand as he tucked the magazine under the counter. "If you'll sign the register, Miss."

"Sign in?" Charley looked toward Marillo.

"New policy. All visitors need to sign in if they go beyond the lobby."

Charley did as she was asked and then followed Marillo into the Sergeant's office. She handed him the envelope of photographs and then sat down in the chair he indicated, across from the desk.

"You could have sent these over, you know," Marillo said, carefully slicing open the envelope. "You didn't have to make a special trip to hand-deliver them."

She shrugged, suspecting Marillo knew full well why she'd brought them herself. She wanted an update on how far he'd gotten in his investigation.

Marillo tutted as he quickly flipped through the photographs. "They're all black and white."

"Well of course they are. We're a newspaper, not *Life* magazine."

Marillo grinned back at her. "I guess that's true. I was hoping, though, that I could see what the paintings looked like in full colour."

"Sorry. This is all I've got."

"It's fine, Mrs. Hall, these will still be useful." He laid out the photographs across his desk. "Was everyone who was at the event photographed?"

"That's Brownie's job and he's particularly good at it. But I left early so I don't know how long he stayed. There is a photo of Jean-Philippe Leloup talking to Mrs. Overstreet, and I know he arrived after I left. I'll ask Brownie if he stuck it out to the bitter end."

"That would be most helpful."

"Since I did this favour for you, perhaps you can tell me where you're at with your investigation."

Marillo raised his head, his eyes narrowed. "This," he

said, waving at the photographs, "is not a *favour*. It is your duty as a citizen to cooperate with the police in a homicide investigation."

She scowled back at him. "You know what I mean. I could have waited until Monday to send these over to you, but I brought them myself, and on a Saturday."

"Which I appreciate." He sat back and crossed his arms over his chest. "All right, Mrs. Hall, what do you want to know?"

"Have you identified the man who was murdered yesterday?"

"We have. His name is Albert Tyson. He was thirty years old and worked as a handyman."

"And the second man in the white van?"

"That would be Stanley Dowden."

"Have you spoken with him? Do you have him in custody?"

"Yes, to both questions, Mrs. Hall."

"Are you going to make me drag every tiny detail out of you?" she snapped.

Marillo chuckled. "It's your interrogation. I don't want to presume to know what information you're looking for."

"Reporters don't interrogate. They interview."

"My apologies. Please proceed with the *interview*."

"Fine!" If he wanted her to treat him like a reluctant source, she would. She had a lot of experience getting people to reveal more than they intended. "How are Mr. Dowden and Mr. Tyson connected?"

"They appear to have been co-workers and friends."

"And did Mr. Dowden tell you who planned the heist?"

"Mr. Tyson, he says."

"Do you believe him?"

"My dear, Mrs. Hall, I don't for a second believe a word

that comes out of a suspect's mouth when his life and liberty are at risk."

"Did he tell you what happened?" And then, anticipating his one-word response, quickly added: "No wait! What did he tell you about what happened yesterday morning?"

Marillo grinned at her catch. He was enjoying this far too much. "According to Mr. Dowden, his friend Mr. Tyson asked to borrow his truck and requested his help to move some things from a job he was working. Mr. Dowden agreed but was miffed when his friend insisted on painting the truck."

"Art G-A-L-L-R-Y."

"Precisely. He said it was going to be a real headache to clean off, but he went along with it anyway."

"And the police costumes?"

"To add to the effect, Mr. Dowden was told. Designed to make it all seem more important."

"Okay, they are in costume and driving the newly painted truck. What then?" she prompted.

"They drove to the Overstreets' home. Tyson knew precisely where the paintings were, and the two of them began loading the artwork into the truck. Dowden said they were already in crates, ready to be shipped, which is what Senator Overstreet told us, too. They're in the middle of the job when a second truck arrives. Dowden was inside, hears Tyson yelling at someone and then gunshots. He runs out and finds Tyson on the ground beside the truck, dead."

"Did he see who shot him?"

"No. He said it was all very confusing. Dowden says the men from the blue truck were rushing toward him and so he took off in his own truck."

Charley chewed the inside of her cheek as she sifted

through what Marillo had told her. Tyson knew exactly where to go and what to take. And when to take it. Clarice had crated up the paintings the night before knowing the gallery would be sending someone in the morning. "Tyson was a handyman, right? Did you check with the Overstreets to see if he'd done work at their home?"

"Gee, Mrs. Hall, the thought never occurred to me," Marillo replied sarcastically.

Okay, she deserved that.

"According to Mrs. Rinehart, Albert Tyson was hired last spring to turn the playroom into an art studio. We sent over a photograph of the deceased and she confirmed it was the same man. The senator said he was aware the work was being done, but as he was in Ottawa during the week, he never saw the workers. Only the bills."

"And Mrs. Overstreet?"

"I haven't been able to speak with her yet. I am hoping to do so later today, provided she is over her shock."

"Did Dowden tell you what they were going to do with the paintings? Were they going to try to sell them?"

Marillo shook his head. "He hasn't said anything more than I've already told you."

Charley eyed Marillo suspiciously. "Why are you being so forthcoming with me about this? Your usual response is 'no comment' when I ask you about a case you're working on."

Marillo beamed at her. "I haven't told you anything that you won't read in your own newspaper this afternoon. While you were enjoying a leisurely breakfast, your fellow newshounds were here at the crack of dawn to get the story."

Leisurely breakfast. If only he knew how un-leisurely her breakfasts had become ever since Evelyn had arrived last fall. Still, the implied rebuke stung. "I told you, I'm not writing about the murder for the paper."

"I know, I know." He held up his hands in mock surrender. "You and Spadina are only looking into the theft."

"Can I speak with Mr. Dowden? I'm assuming he's back in the cells."

"Are you his lawyer?"

"No, of course not."

"Then no, you can't speak with him."

She blew out her frustration. "Can you tell me anything about him, then? What kind of man would agree to help perpetrate a crime and then leave his friend to die alone?"

Marillo shrugged. "You got me. He said Tyson was already dead when he fled. The medical examiner concurs, says death was likely immediate."

"You have the autopsy report already?"

"The preliminary," Marillo said. "The full report will arrive sometime next week."

"Does the preliminary report give the calibre of the bullet that killed him?"

"No comment."

Charley recognized the tone. Marillo wasn't going to divulge anything more to her. She thanked him and left.

She was going to be late for her next appointment, but at least part of the mystery seemed to have been solved. Tyson must have assumed Clarice's paintings were valuable —maybe he'd heard they were going to be shown in a gallery —and tried to steal them expecting to make money from them. Had he been intending to sell them or hold them for ransom? In any event, he had the means and motive. It was too bad for him that someone else did as well.

"It's about time you got here." Mark rose from the plush blue and gold brocade chair in the lobby of the city's finest hotel. A deep trench ran between his dark eyebrows and his jaw was clenched as he stalked towards her. "Check-out is in less than thirty minutes."

She squared her shoulders and raised her chin, unwilling to allow him to make her feel guilty. She hadn't deliberately kept him waiting. Her conversation with Marillo had gone longer than she'd anticipated. But she'd gotten some good information from him, which she'd share with Mark once he calmed down.

"Sorry. I was delayed. He's still here, isn't he?"

"Yes, no thanks to you. The art gallery's truck arrived thirty minutes ago to pick him up and take him back to Toronto. I paid the driver to circle the city a few times and come back at noon."

"How very creative of you." She walked past him and punched the button for the elevator.

Charley's second meeting with Lee Rothko confirmed her initial impression of him. He was an odd little man, but the little was in height only. Rothko was a good three inches shorter than her five-foot-seven self and his portly frame gave him the illusion of looking as wide as he was tall. His closely cropped dark hair and clean-shaven face both emphasized his puffed-out cheeks and triple chins. His tailored, black, double-breasted suit jacket hung open revealing a satin, burgundy-coloured vest into which was tucked a flamboyant yellow and green floral necktie with a pearl and diamond stickpin. She thought back to their meeting with Jean-Philippe Leloup yesterday and concluded there was something a little eccentric about all these artsy types. Clarice didn't seem to fit the mould.

"I don't have a lot of time. I expected my truck to be here by now." He glanced at his watch. "I am due to check out any minute."

"We won't keep you too long," Mark said in a reassuring tone. "As you are aware, Senator Overstreet has engaged me to recover the missing paintings. I'm sure that would be of interest to you and your gallery, too." Mark smoothly eased the man out of the way so he and Charley could enter his suite.

Charley glanced around the room. It was exquisitely furnished. A royal-blue, velvet tufted sofa was situated beneath a wide window, with two matching armchairs on either side. A rich mahogany coffee table sat on a lush woven carpet of navy and gold. Rather than paintings, the walls were adorned with large historical photographs of the city—probably for the best, Charley thought, given how subjective one's opinion of art could be. On the sidebar was a pair of decanters which she assumed contained sherry and brandy, judging by the crystal glasses beside them. The brandy seemed to have been well-sampled. Through the door to a second room, she could see an enormous unmade bed and a large, brown leather suitcase lying open on top.

The view from the room was of the city's skyline rather than the lakefront. Icy, snow-covered Lake Ontario made a bleak impression this time of year, so it was the canny patron who saved his pennies and took the "lesser" city view.

Rothko closed the door behind them. He pulled a pocket watch from his vest and wound it nervously. "I am at your disposal, ah...what did you say your name was again?"

"Detective Spadina. And this is Mrs. Hall. I believe you met her at the *vernissage.*"

"Did I?" He squinted at her. "Well, it's nice to see you again, then, Mrs. Hall."

"Let me get right to the point, Mr. Rothko," Mark said. "How was it that your gallery was selected to exhibit Mrs. Overstreet's paintings. From what I understand, a gallery in Montreal would have been more appropriate. I'm from Toronto so I know how conservative the town can be."

"It seems a brave choice," Charley added.

"Yes, well, brave. That's me." Rothko put the watch back into his vest pocket.

Charley and Mark waited for him to say more. She knew he was reluctant to explain, but she also knew that keeping their silence would unnerve the gallery owner and hopefully get him to open up.

Finally, Rothko heaved a sigh. "All right, fine. Yes, I was very reluctant to exhibit Mrs. Overstreet's works at first. I didn't know how they'd be received, and I was afraid I was risking my reputation by representing them."

"So, you didn't seek her out?" Charley asked.

"No. Her husband, the senator, asked me to mount an exhibition. He brought one of the paintings to show me and had photographs of the rest of the collection."

"It wasn't Mrs. Overstreet who contacted you?" Mark asked.

"I never met her until the other night. All my dealings have been with the senator."

"You said you were reluctant at first. What made you change your mind and decide to show them?" Charley asked.

Rothko lowered his head and toed the carpet.

"You didn't, did you?" Mark said. "Senator Overstreet is footing the bill for all of this, isn't that right?"

Rothko's head shot up. "I'm not happy about it, but art is a tricky business. It's hard for a middle-sized gallery like mine to succeed."

"He had to have offered more than simply paying your expenses for you to put your reputation at risk, as you say," Mark pressed.

"He's also giving me an eighty percent commission on any sales, plus the exclusive right to represent future paintings if she's successful," Rothko said quietly.

"Eighty percent?" Charley whistled. "That's high isn't it?"

"Unheard of," Rothko agreed. "Frankly, I was still skeptical that anyone was going to come to see them, let alone make an offer to buy one, and that was fine with me. I planned to promote the collection as little as possible." He reached into a briefcase that rested against the sofa and handed them each a coloured bulletin. "The senator is a powerful man. I had these made up so he couldn't accuse me of not doing my job. I almost died when I saw Leloup at the *vernissage* Thursday night. Never in my wildest dreams did I expect him to come all the way to Toronto for an unknown artist."

"So, he came to Kingston instead," Mark said.

"It was supposed to be *private*—friends and family only."

Charley paced toward the window, which looked down onto the street in front of the hotel. The truck from Rothko's gallery was easing up to the curb in front of the building. She stared at the bulletin in her hand. Underneath the gallery's name and the dates for the exhibit was a large full-coloured photograph of one of the paintings in Clarice's collection. If Leloup had seen this, why would he have bothered to come from almost two hundred miles away to view something he thought was amateurish? And with a threatening snowstorm?

Maybe the senator paid him, too.

When she turned back, Rothko was handing Mark the remaining bulletins from his bag. "Give these to the senator, would you? I will get more made up and sent out, but perhaps he can circulate them among his friends and acquaintances in Ottawa."

"I thought you didn't want to promote Mrs. Overstreet's paintings," Charley said.

"That was before they were stolen." Rothko stepped past her to look out the window. "Oh good. My truck is here. I am anxious to get home so I can start promoting the exhibition."

"I don't understand," Mark said. "What are you promoting? The paintings have been stolen."

"Exactly, and once they are found everyone will be clamouring to see what was so special about them. There's nothing like a little notoriety to add interest."

"You expect them to be found?" Charley asked. "I thought most stolen works of art are never recovered."

"That's not, in fact, true," Rothko said, slipping his arms into the sleeves of his dark wool coat. "Besides, we're talking about an unknown artist. It's not like Clarice Overstreet is Rembrandt or even Picasso." He put a felt hat on his head and went into his bedroom to collect his suitcase. "The theft of her paintings is the best thing that could have happened to me."

CHARLEY SLUMPED down in the passenger seat of Mark's black sedan. She'd started to tell him about what she'd learned from Detective Marillo only to have him inform her that he already knew it all. He'd had breakfast with the cop and then sat in on the briefing Marillo had given to the press. If she didn't know better, she'd suspect a conspiracy between the two of them to keep her off her game.

The early bird gets the worm, Mark had quipped. The truth of that irked her as much as losing her scoop.

But it was Saturday and while she could get away with claiming work responsibilities for skipping family breakfasts during the week, Gran was insistent Charley join them on the weekend. Even Freddie had started to comply with the edict, although Charley wasn't sure if it was Gran or Evelyn he was most concerned about offending.

"Do you think it's possible Rothko orchestrated the theft?" Charley asked.

"Definitely not the first one. He seems too certain that the paintings will be recovered, so if he was involved at all, it would have to be with the second team of thieves. But even that I dou— " Mark swerved sharply to avoid a pedestrian, sending Charley sliding along the seat and crashing into him. "Sorry about that," he muttered as she scuttled back to her side of the car.

"The city's slow to clean the sidewalks so everyone's walking on the roads," Charley said, remembering her own close call on the way to the police station earlier that morning. "Someone's going to get killed."

"You should take it up with your alderman." Mark chuckled. "As I was saying, Rothko only profits if the paintings—and presumably the thieves—*are* found. He seems far too calm for someone who could be facing a murder charge."

She wasn't as convinced by the gallery owner's untroubled demeanour. There was something shady about him. Plus, he'd already admitted his reputation could be bought. How much more would Clarice's paintings be worth after the theft? If Rothko was the type of man who didn't care if anyone got hurt, or in this case killed, what would stop him from getting rid of the second set of thieves, too?

Mark turned into the long driveway leading to the Overstreets' home and parked the car under the carriage porch. He'd invited her to go along with him to give the senator a progress report and Charley was hopeful that, as a woman, she'd succeed where the police had so far failed, and Clarice would agree to see her.

Mrs. Rinehart told Mark to wait in the senator's office and led Charley up the spiral staircase to the landing where she asked her to wait while she checked to see if Mrs. Overstreet was willing to receive visitors.

Loud, angry voices—a man and a woman—arose from behind the closed French doors across the landing. Mrs. Rinehart glanced back at Charley, her eyes wide in alarm.

Before either of them could react, the doors flung open and Senator Overstreet stomped out of the room. He paused when he saw Charley. "Maybe you can talk some sense into her," he bit out before marching down the stairs.

"His hand," Charley said, stupidly. She'd noticed it was bandaged. An odd thing to focus on considering what she'd witnessed.

"He burned it in the fireplace the other day," Mrs. Rinehart said.

"I noticed he was wearing gloves yesterday. He said he was cold, but the room..." Why was she even pursuing this? She could see Clarice staring at her from inside her suite. "Never mind." Charley walked past the housekeeper to the doorway and waited to be allowed into the room.

Clarice nodded and motioned her in. As Charley turned back from closing the doors, Clarice rushed to her and wrapped her arms around her waist. "Oh, Mrs. Hall, I don't know what I'm going to do."

Charley helped her over to the *chaise-longue* in front of the enormous three-panelled window that looked out over the carriage porch at the front of the house. She kept her arm around Clarice and allowed her to sob quietly into her shoulder. It was easy to forget how young she was. When Clarice was hosting the *vernissage* the other evening, she had seemed perfectly poised and in her element as the lady of the manor and shining star of the event. Today, though, she was like a lost child. Her flaxen-coloured hair hung limply around her shoulders and she was still in an ivory-coloured cotton nightdress. When she gazed up at Charley, her hazel eyes were puffy and red, as was her petite nose.

"I know how hard it must be to have something so personal taken from you," Charley said, rubbing small circles across Clarice's back. "But I am optimistic we will find your paintings. And Mr. Rothko says the theft may even work to your advantage."

"No!" Clarice buried her head again and continued mumbling but it was unintelligible to Charley.

Charley eased her back. "There, there. It can't be as bad as all that."

"I never wanted to exhibit my paintings," Clarice said between great gulping sobs. "It's all Harold's doing. He wouldn't listen to me...insisted on showing them to everyone."

Charley spotted a decanter of brandy across the room. Getting up, she went and poured a small glass for Clarice. "Here," she said, sitting back down beside the young woman. "Now, why shouldn't you be recognized for your talents? Meredith Cannon thinks your paintings are quite brilliant—extraordinary, even—and she has been to some of the greatest galleries in Europe."

"You don't understand. He isn't doing it for me. He is doing it for himself, to justify all the time he spends away."

"I'm sorry." Charley didn't know what else to say.

Clarice dabbed at her eyes with a handkerchief. "I guess I brought it on myself. I didn't listen when others warned me what it would be like to be a politician's wife."

"That's no excuse for his behaviour."

"It's probably for the best that they're gone. Now he can't force me into that awful exhibition."

"Will you continue painting?"

"I don't know." Clarice took a sip of her brandy. "No, probably not. I'll have to find something else to occupy my time."

"I hate to ask you this, but the police are going to ask you later, anyway, so maybe this will help you be prepared." Charley winced at how self-serving she sounded. "How much has your husband told you about what happened yesterday? Did you know there were two groups of thieves?"

"Yes, he told me that."

"And one man was shot."

Clarice gasped and paled. "Yes."

"I'm sorry to tell you that the man was Albert Tyson."

Clarice seemed to hold her breath as she shook her head. "I don't know him," she said, finally exhaling.

"He was a handyman. He built your art studio," Charley continued.

"Did he? I don't remember. This has all been quite overwhelming." Clarice stood. "If you don't mind, Mrs. Hall, I'd like to be alone now. Will you please show yourself out?"

Out on the landing, Charley leaned against the French doors, forcing herself to unball her fists while she took several deep breaths to calm herself. She was so angry with the senator right now, she'd likely say something she'd regret later.

Kill them with kindness, not knives. Charley repeated Gran's mantra.

Clarice had been so young when she married the senator. An older man, handsome and powerful, he'd probably turned her head with promises of a grand future. For a waitress struggling to make ends meet, she must have felt as if she'd fallen into a fairy tale. But fairy tales are not real life. Clarice had to move to a new city—a new province—where she knew no one and was then abandoned for days or weeks at a time while Overstreet continued on as he always had.

Kindness not knives. Kindness not knives.

Better hide the cutlery.

⸎ ⸎

THE DOOR to the senator's office was closed, which was for the best. Charley didn't want to see him. She'd wait for Mark in the foyer.

She heard a woman's laughter coming from where she was heading. It was followed by the low rumble of a man's voice. She paused, recognizing both, and then chastised herself for being foolish. Why should she care if Mark and Poppy were together, laughing or whatever they were doing? Still, she was hesitant to join them. She took a sharp turn down another hallway, making her way to the kitchen, her nose picking up the scent of baking bread as she approached.

Was it strange that Clarice hadn't recognized the name of the dead man? Mark wouldn't think so. He'd claim that it was yet another example of the elitist attitudes of the upper classes toward those who worked for them. But Clarice wasn't from a privileged background. And it was her art studio that he'd been working on. But that had been months ago. Could Charley name every handyman that had done work for her family over the past few years? Probably not. It was generally the housekeeper who made those arrangements.

"Charley! I mean Mrs. Hall." Mrs. Rinehart flushed at her gaffe.

"I like Charley better. It makes me feel old to be called Mrs. Hall." She took a seat at the weathered wooden table where the housekeeper was sorting through a hill of currants, looking for stems.

"Imagine how old I must feel."

Charley shook her head. "You've barely aged."

"*Pshaw*, with you." Mrs. Rinehart battered away the compliment. "Can I pour you a cup of tea? The kettle's hot."

"I'll get it." Although it had been well over a decade since she'd been in the Overstreets' kitchen, Charley was comforted to find things where she remembered them to be. "I understand the man who was killed yesterday did some work here," she said as she prepared her cup.

"Mr. Tyson. Yes. Such a terrible thing."

"Did you arrange for him to do the work on the art studio?" Charley resumed her seat.

"He was recommended to me. I checked his references and they were all excellent." She sounded defensive.

"I wasn't suggesting you should have known he'd turn out to be a thief," Charley said quickly. "I was simply wondering how involved Mrs. Overstreet was in the renovation. She didn't seem to recognize his name when I asked her upstairs."

"She didn't?" Mrs. Rinehart's perfectly shaped eyebrows rose sharply. "Well, it was some time ago."

"But it was her studio. Surely, she had opinions on what she wanted to be done with it."

Mrs. Rinehart shrugged and returned to picking through the currants. "I'm sure she did. I certainly couldn't be expected to know her mind or what passes for an art studio these days."

Charley sipped her tea. "When you spoke to the police, did they tell you anything else about what had happened?" she asked. It was unlikely, but sometimes the police let slip some additional information to the family that they kept from the public.

"I haven't spoken with them at all."

Charley thumped her teacup down on the table. "But I thought you were the one who told them about Albert Tyson."

"They called the senator and he asked me about it. He

was the one they spoke with." Mrs. Rinehart kept her head cast down, focusing on her task.

"And they haven't interviewed you at all?"

"I suppose they assume since I wasn't at the event, I have nothing to add."

There was something in the tone of Mrs. Rinehart's response that made Charley think she knew more than she was letting on. "Do you have anything? To add, I mean."

A range of emotions cross the housekeeper's face, but Charley didn't push her. Mrs. Rinehart was silent for a good while, likely trying to decide how much to share. A lifetime in domestic service had taught her the importance of discretion.

Finally, she stopped her sorting and raised her gaze to Charley's. "I told the senator about this, but he says it's not important. He didn't think the police would be interested."

"Can you tell me?"

"It was close to midnight. The *vernissage* had ended early, of course, due to the storm. Everyone had been gone for several hours and the family had retired for the evening." She had started sorting through the currants again. "I was doing my rounds, making sure the caterers had tidied up properly when someone came to the door."

"Was it someone for the event? Were they delayed by the storm?"

Mrs. Rinehart looked up and smiled. "You always did ask so many questions as a child. I am glad you have been able to find a useful outlet for that proclivity. No, it was a gentleman who said he'd been at the *vernissage* earlier and had discovered, once he'd returned home, that he'd lost a cuff link. He said it held great sentimental value and asked if he could come in and search for it."

"It must have been very important to him if he was prepared to travel back through that snowstorm."

"I told him it was far too late to let him in the house and that if he left me his name and telephone number, I would search for the item and let him know if I found it. He refused and insisted I let him in. I told him he was free to return in the morning and bolted the door."

"Good for you. Did he come back?"

"I haven't seen him since."

"And I'm assuming you haven't found a cuff link," Charley said.

"No."

"Well, I suppose it's possible he found it himself," Charley mused. "What did he look like? Did you recognize him at all?"

"No, I'm quite certain I've never seen him before."

"Can you tell me anything about him?"

"Only that he was foreign. He spoke with an accent."

"What kind of accent?"

Mrs. Rinehart shrugged. "I don't know. It was a little familiar, but not quite."

"There you are!" Mark said from the doorway. "What are you doing back here?"

"Yes, I was going to ask the very same thing." Poppy squeezed past him.

Mrs. Rinehart jumped up from her chair and looked guiltily at the new arrivals.

Charley swallowed her irritation at the untimely interruption and stood. She rested her hand on the older woman's shoulder to reassure her. "We were catching up. It's nothing for you to worry about, Poppy. I've long given up trying to convince Mrs. Rinehart to leave your family for mine." Charley picked up her teacup and took it to the sink.

"I think I've kept you long enough, Mrs. Rinehart. We can show ourselves out."

Without looking at either Poppy or Mark, Charley left the kitchen and headed straight toward the foyer. The less time she spent in Poppy's company the better. She hoped Mark was ready to leave, too. Otherwise, she'd brave the treacherous roads on foot.

"No, not that way," Mark said, taking her arm. "That's why I was looking for you. Detective Marillo is here. He wants to see everyone—including us."

DETECTIVE MARILLO WAS ALONE in the senator's study. He turned back from warming his hands in front of the fire as they entered the room. "Your father has gone to get your mother," he said to Poppy.

"*Step*-mother."

"Of course." He turned to Charley and Mark. "I tried to see Lee Rothko this morning, but he's already left town."

"Is that right?" Mark feigned innocence.

Charley wondered why Mark didn't want Marillo to know they'd seen the gallery owner a few hours earlier. She thought they'd become friends but maybe, as a former detective himself, Mark felt some rivalry with Marillo. And he never missed an opportunity to disparage the Kingston Police Department, believing them to be inferior to the larger Toronto one he'd left.

"I'm sorry, she's not coming." Senator Overstreet shuffled into the room, looking as if his world was ending. "This has been so hard on her."

"That's all right, Senator. I thought I might have been able to give her some news."

"You found the paintings?" Charley asked.

"We've found what we believe is the blue delivery truck. It's severely burned, but I was hoping Mrs. Overstreet would accompany me to identify some of what we've recovered."

"Oh, I am quite certain she's not up to doing that, Detective," Overstreet said.

"I could go," Charley volunteered. "I've seen the paintings and I do think it would be better, Senator, if you stayed here with Clarice."

"I would be most grateful to you, Charley." Overstreet looked relieved.

"We'll follow you, then," Mark said to Marillo.

"I could go, too," Poppy said. "I've seen the paintings."

"Thank you, Mrs. Tremblay, but we need to limit the number of people at the scene," Marillo said.

"It's important we don't disturb the area any more than necessary," Mark explained.

"Well, I should go instead of Charley. After all, I am family." Poppy took Mark's arm and gazed up at him. "It should be me."

Marillo looked uncomfortably toward the senator, as if expecting him to arbitrate the dispute, but he was frowning at the fireplace.

Mark patted Poppy's arm. "Charley has more experience at crime scenes. Besides, it's not as glamorous as it sounds. It's bound to be messy. And if there's a fire, we may find bodies in the wreckage. I don't know if you've ever smelled burning flesh, but it's something you never forget. I wouldn't wish that on you."

Poppy recoiled at the mention of burning flesh. "No, you're right of course. I was trying to be helpful."

"Of course, you were. That is your nature." Mark said.

Oh, brother.

It took an extreme effort, but Charley managed to not roll her eyes at the two of them. Poppy was no shrinking violet and Mark was no solicitous gentleman trying to protect her. They were each playing some sort of game with the other. Mark loved games.

There would be no dead bodies at the scene. If there had been, Marillo would have directly gone there himself and sent a junior officer to collect them. But charred corpses aside, what bothered Charley about the exchange was the seemingly tacit agreement by everyone that her feminine nasal sensibilities were somehow less precious than Poppy's.

"What were you really talking to the housekeeper about?" Mark asked as he pulled onto the street to follow Marillo's vehicle.

"I told you, we were catching up. It's been a few years since I've seen her."

"That's not your style, though, is it? Chatting with the help, I mean."

Charley grimaced at the rebuke. He'd said as much before, and although she disagreed, it stung, nevertheless. "She was wonderful to us when we were children, almost like a mother. Why are you so suspicious?"

"Why are you so evasive? We're a team, aren't we?" He glanced over at her, but she wouldn't meet his gaze. He sighed and returned his focus to the road. "All right then, since you don't want to talk about Mrs. Rinehart, what did Clarice tell you?"

"Only that she's terribly unhappy. She never wanted to exhibit her paintings. The senator forced her into it."

"And the dead handyman?"

"That was a little odd. She said she didn't recognize the name. I asked Mrs. Rinehart about it since it's possible she and not Clarice dealt with Tyson." Charley bit the inside of her cheek. She was certain the housekeeper had been holding something back. "Initially, she seemed surprised by Clarice's denial, but then she admitted it was quite a while ago, and well, you know how my class deals with the help." She couldn't resist the barb.

"Clarice wasn't of your class, though, was she?" Mark refused to rise to the bait. "She was a waitress who'd been elevated to the lady of the manor."

"Which may be why she left the work to Mrs. Rinehart to coordinate."

"But it was her art studio."

Charley stared out the window. Mark wasn't raising any questions she wasn't already mulling around.

"She strikes me as a gold digger."

Charley whirled in her seat to face him. "Why would you think that?"

"I spoke with the senator. He's genuinely smitten with his young wife and beside himself with worry for her."

"Not worried enough to take her to Ottawa with him."

"I'm not convinced the rumours of his infidelity Meredith told us about are true."

"Those rumours weren't new to me. Everyone knew his first marriage was an unhappy one."

"But that doesn't mean he's unfaithful to his second wife. Don't you think her reaction to the theft of a few paintings a little cockeyed?"

She bristled. "They weren't just a few paintings to her." Charley knew what it was like to give her heart and soul to a project and have it taken away. She'd come to terms with losing her place on the city beat, but at the time, she'd been devastated. "I think your opinion of Clarice is being influenced by all the time you've been spending with Poppy."

"What does Poppy have to do with anything?" He eased his sedan to a stop behind Marillo's.

"She is married, you know."

"So?" He turned to her.

"And she has two children."

"Careful, Tiger, that's starting to sound like jealousy."

"Don't be ridiculous." Charley pushed open the passenger door and stepped into a knee-high snowbank.

Great!

"It's right up ahead," Marillo said, helping her climb through the bank of snow as she rounded to the front of Mark's car. "The men have almost finished photographing and measuring everything but watch where you're stepping anyway."

Further along the road, where Marillo indicated, was the blue delivery truck lying on its side, peeking out of the snow partway down an embankment. Snow-filled ruts showed its trajectory off the road. As she approached, she noticed splashes of red paint marking the faint foot holes that led away from the truck and up to the road, where they disappeared. "They were picked up by someone," she said.

"Yeah, we're not sure if it was an accomplice or a good Samaritan," Marillo said.

"No dead bodies, I presume."

"None," Marillo said while Mark chuckled behind them.

She ignored Mark's outstretched hand to help her step over the snowbank, which seemed to amuse him more. "Can you tell if the fire was the result of landing in the ditch or deliberately set?" she asked Marillo.

"It was deliberate. The back of the vehicle is charred not the engine."

"Where the paintings would have been." Had the

thieves wanted to destroy the artwork because of the accident, or had it been their plan all along?

Mark had scaled down the embankment and was peering into the van. "There are no paintings here," he called up.

"Ah, that's the interesting part. They're over there." Marillo pointed toward a wooded area about fifty feet away.

The fire had died some time ago, but there were enough ash and bits and pieces of canvas and wood framing to indicate that it must have been the whole collection that had been sent up in flames.

Charley picked up a branch. "May I?" she asked Marillo.

"Sure. My guys have photographed it. They'll start collecting the pieces as soon as they're done with the truck."

Charley poked at a few of the larger pieces and flipped one over. Clarice's signature was visible over the multicoloured splashes of green, red, and orange on the remaining piece of canvas.

"Do you think there's enough ash and debris to account for all four of the paintings?" Mark asked Marillo.

"Why?"

"What if the thieves knew they couldn't move all of the paintings after they lost their truck and so they decided to keep one or two for themselves and destroy the rest?" Mark shrugged. "If we could figure out why they took the collection in the first place, we might be closer to identifying who they are. Knowing whether they destroyed all the paintings or kept a few might help. That's all."

"We'll take a closer look when we get it all back to the station."

"Do we know when all this happened?" Charley asked.

"Probably yesterday morning, shortly after the theft, given how much snow is on the van."

"The fire pit was protected by the trees," she said.

"Yeah, a lucky break for us."

Or deliberate.

"You'll let us know if you find out anything more when you take the bits of the paintings back to the station, right?" Mark asked.

"Sure, if you'll let me know if you find out anything, too."

"Of course," Mark replied.

Mark held open the driver's side door of his car so Charley could slide across into the passenger seat. He didn't immediately start the engine but danced his fingers along the steering wheel. "I think we can rule out Rothko as the mastermind of the theft," he mused. "Even if the thieves kept a couple of the paintings, he wouldn't have benefited without the whole collection." He paused, but when she didn't respond, he continued: "Given how everyone feels about art in general, I'd say whoever did this didn't have a strong affinity for the paintings. Maybe it was, as Meredith suggested, someone who didn't want to see the two branches of Abstract Expressionism united."

Charley continued to stare out the front window, watching Marillo give final instructions to his men before driving away.

"Is there something on your mind, Tiger?" Mark tapped her on the shoulder.

She should have told him about what Mrs. Rinehart had said about the foreigner, but she was reluctant to do so. Mark and Marillo had promised to keep one another in the loop, but she felt alienated from the two of them, like a third arm they were forced to bring along but had no real use for.

Everything about this case unsettled her, but she couldn't figure out why. She'd dealt with thieves and murderers before. They didn't scare her. Usually, the chase of a good story sent her blood racing with anticipation as she tracked down every clue to solve the mystery. Why was this one different? She could hardly wait until it was resolved, and she could put it all out of her mind.

At one time, she'd felt like a member of the Overstreet family. Although the first Mrs. Overstreet was rarely around, Mrs. Rinehart had welcomed her and made her feel wanted in a way none of her grandmother's housekeepers ever had. And Charley had adored the senator. He was younger than grandpa and so she'd often imagined that the time he spent with her and the other children was what it would have been like had her father been alive. Finding out how poorly the senator treated his new wife upset Charley a great deal.

And then there was Poppy.

When their friendship had ended so, too, had her ties with the Overstreet family. No one, not even Mrs. Rinehart or the senator had sought her out, followed her career, cheered her on. She'd been reminded all over again that it was Poppy and not her who belonged.

Jealous?

Maybe, but not in the way Mark suggested.

She turned her head to look out the side window. "Can you drive me home, please?"

"Don't think for one second that you're fooling me, Charlotte," Bessie Stormont said as she hung her heavy tweed coat on a hook in the cloakroom of Sydenham Street's Gothic-style church. Originally built by Methodists in the previous century, the congregation became part of the United Church of Canada when three Protestant denominations merged in 1925. "I know you're up to something."

Charley sat down on the bench to remove her boots, unwilling to meet Gran's eyes. "You know what they say about not looking a gift horse in the mouth."

"That didn't work out very well for King Priam, did it?"

Charley's head shot up. "Are you accusing me of being a Trojan horse?" She grinned.

"If the saddle fits," Bessie chuckled.

Charley had thought her last-minute request to join the Imperial Order Daughters of the Empire's knitting circle that afternoon would delight her grandmother. After all, she'd been trying for eons to convince Charley to become a member of the charitable organization. But Gran was canny, and her suspicions weren't unwarranted. Charley had wanted to show Mrs. Rinehart the photographs from the *vernissage* to see if she could identify the "foreigner," but Sunday was her day off and she'd volunteered at her church to help prepare tea and sandwiches for the IODE.

Although she hadn't touched her knitting needles in over four years, Charley was pleased with how quickly her fingers remembered the stitches to manipulate the three needles to make hats and mittens for the city's unfortunate. She glanced around the community hall, recognizing most of the women there. Charley was the only one in the room under fifty. With the war over, the younger women who'd participated before were now home with their husbands, raising their children.

Children. That was something Charley hadn't given much thought to. She hadn't needed to while Theo was fighting, and then missing, in Europe. Now that Freddie had confirmed he wasn't coming home, there would be an expectation for her to remarry and have babies. She was thirty, after all. Spinster age to many.

Except she didn't feel like a spinster.

And she didn't feel like having children. At least not yet. Probably better to find a husband first.

She wasn't sure how much she wanted one of those, either.

She knew, though, if she waited too long, it would be too late. Poppy already had two school-aged children and she wasn't unique among their classmates. And now that Dan was married, how long would it be before he announced that Meredith was pregnant? That was news Charley both welcomed and dreaded.

She had hoped that seeing Dan married would extinguish some of the longings she still felt for him. But it hadn't seemed to make any difference. Maybe knowing he and his wife were having a baby would do the trick.

And if it didn't?

"Charlotte!"

Gran's voice startled her, and she jerked back. "Oh darn. Now I've dropped a stitch." She deftly caught it with a needle and slid it back where it belonged.

"Are you feeling all right? You've been staring into space for the past five minutes."

"Yes, I'm fine, Gran." She stood up, suddenly restless. "I think I'm going to go for a walk to stretch my legs." She put her needles with their half-formed blue-and-white-striped toque down onto her chair.

"Ah, yes, here comes Odysseus and his troops, now," Gran said, pointing a needle at the manila-coloured enve-lope Charley had taken out of her knitting bag. "Charge!"

***

CHARLEY PUSHED OPEN the swinging door into the church's kitchen. In addition to Mrs. Rinehart, Charley recognized the minister's wife arranging an assortment of sandwiches and cookies onto a row of plates. Both women looked up and then nodded for her to come in.

"Hello, Mrs. Hall," Mrs. Gallagher said. "Are they ready for us?"

"No, not yet," Charley said, snagging an oatmeal cookie off the nearest plate. "Probably another twenty minutes. I think there's more gossip than knitting going on."

"As ever." Mrs. Gallagher grinned. "Still, it's nice to see so many coming together to help the poor in our community."

"You wanted to show me some photos?" Mrs. Rinehart said. "I think we're all set here, Mrs. Gallagher. Is it all right if I take a wee break with Ch—ah, Mrs. Hall?"

"Of course, dear. Take a cup of tea and some cookies into the reverend's study. I can finish up the rest."

Charley turned on the desk lamp in the dim study and sat down on the sofa beside Mrs. Rinehart. She handed her the envelope. "These were taken by the *Trib*'s photographer that night."

Mrs. Rinehart withdrew the stack of photographs and began to scan each of them, handing them back to Charley, one after another.

"Do you still have your camera?" Charley asked.

"Oh, no." Mrs. Rinehart shook her head. "I haven't used it for many years. I'm not even sure where it is anymore."

"That's too bad. I remember you snapping photos of us kids all the time. I still have some of the ones you gave me to share with Gran and Grandpa."

"The senator and the first Mrs. Overstreet were away so much of the time; I didn't want them to miss their children's special moments."

"You showed me your darkroom in the cellar, once. Remember?"

"Yes, I remember. You were so excited to see the images emerge in the developer solution. You thought I could do magic."

"I still do when I consider how efficiently you run that household. Oh, that's Jean-Philippe Leloup," Charley said, pointing out the art critic who was chatting with Clarice in front of one of the large canvases. "He's from Montreal and has a French-Canadian accent."

Mrs. Rinehart raised her gaze to Charley's and arched an imperial eyebrow. "I do know what a French-Canadian accent sounds like. And a France French one, too, for that matter. The senator has had visitors from many countries over the years. The accent that gentleman had wasn't anything I'd heard before."

"Of course." Charley should have known better. French accents were quite common in Canada—even in the predominantly English city of Kingston.

Charley had prided herself on being able to recognize accents, too, but there was one she'd come across recently that had stumped her. And he had been at the *vernissage*, although she'd managed to avoid him. She rifled through the photographs Mrs. Rinehart had returned to her and then examined the remainder more carefully as the older woman continued to look for the foreigner among the guests.

He's not here.

Charley accepted the final photo from Mrs. Rinehart.

How had he managed to not be photographed?

"Are you familiar with Colin Banks?" Charley asked.

"I've seen his name in the newspaper."

"He's becoming a prominent member of the Liberal party. Perhaps he's been to see the senator?"

Mrs. Rinehart puckered her lips as she considered. "Not to the house in Kingston. I keep careful records of all the senator's visitors. Perhaps they met in Ottawa. Why?"

"He's from South Africa and has a distinctive accent. He was there that night. I don't know why Brownie didn't get a picture of him." Charley blew out a puff of frustration and stuffed the photos back into the envelope. She'd have to have a chat with the *Trib*'s photographer.

Colin Banks. Meredith's brother and Dan's political backer. Charley didn't like him or trust him. She hadn't been able to find anything to suggest the man was crooked, although she was fairly certain he'd made a veiled threat to her at Dan's wedding—insinuating that if she looked too closely at Dan, she might not like what she saw. She'd known Dan her whole life, so if there was something to "see" now, she knew it would be a result of his involvement with Colin. She'd promised both Dan and Meredith she wouldn't actively investigate Colin, and she'd keep to her word. But all bets were off if she stumbled across something. Then she'd pursue him right to the front page of the *Kingston Tribune.*

"I'm sorry I can't be more help," Mrs. Rinehart said, picking up her teacup.

"I'll find a photo of Colin Banks, but if it's not him, I think you should tell Detective Marillo about your late-night caller," Charley said.

"Oh dear, I can't go against the senator's wishes."

"At least talk to the senator about it," Charley pressed. "Can I ask you a few more questions about the work Mr. Tyson did?" When Mrs. Rinehart nodded, she continued. "How long did he work for you? Did he do work other than the playroom?"

"Well, that's the thing. It seemed to take a lot longer than I would have thought. But perhaps it was because he was doing other work, too."

"What do you mean?"

Mrs. Rinehart took a sip of her tea, delaying her response, and a furrow formed between her eyebrows. "He'd often arrive at odd hours, sometimes after I retired for the evening."

"And work on the studio at night?"

A pink flush stained Mrs. Rinehart's cheeks. Her hand trembled slightly, and she put down her teacup.

It slowly dawned on Charley what the woman was not saying. "Are you telling me Clarice and Tyson were lovers?"

Mrs. Rinehart rose. "I really must be getting back. Mrs. Gallagher must be almost ready to serve the tea." She placed their empty teacups and the plate of uneaten cookies on the tray, picked it up and headed for the door.

"One more thing," Charley called to her. That bandaged hand. Those burned canvases. "Did the senator go out at all on Friday, after the theft? Or any other time?"

Mrs. Rinehart paused but didn't turn around. "No. He's been at home ever since he returned from Ottawa on Thursday afternoon."

CHARLEY SLAMMED the telephone receiver down into its cradle. "Darn it!"

"Rough day?" Grace asked before placing a steaming mug down on the desk. "Maybe this will help. It's the last of that special tea you gave me at Christmas."

"Thanks." Charley took a sip of the cinnamon and spice blend. It was meant to be calming, but she doubted anything could soothe her nerves today.

Grace perched on the edge of her desk and picked up the coloured bulletin promoting Clarice's Toronto exhibition. "I think I prefer it in black and white," she said, scrutinizing the page.

"Me, too." Charley grinned back at her. The tea might not improve her mood, but Grace always found a way to sand down the rough edges of the day.

"So, what's got you so steamed anyway?" the archivist asked.

"Nobody's answering their phone, that's all. I need to talk to Brownie about the photos from the *vernissage*."

"Sherman has him down at city works taking photographs of the mounds of snow the clean-up crews dumped there after the storm last week."

Charley rolled her eyes imagining that front-page photo. "Great."

"And who else?" Grace prompted.

"Mark. We're supposed to be working on this art theft together." She'd called him yesterday, as soon as she'd gotten home from the IODE knitting circle, but he'd brushed her off saying he had plans and would catch up with her soon. He wouldn't tell her what those plans were, but she had a suspicion they had something to do with Poppy. And today, he wasn't answering his telephone at all.

"I can't help you with that. He was supposed to come for Sunday dinner, yesterday, but he called at the last minute to cancel. No explanation. But then, that's Mark isn't it?"

"If you mean rude and inconsiderate, yes, that's him exactly."

Grace giggled. "That's not what I meant, Charley. It's that he's not one to be a slave to tradition and social convention. I think it's because he was raised in an orphanage and has been on his own for so long."

"You're far more charitable than I am."

"What are you working on for this weekend's women's pages?" Grace asked, changing the subject. "Can I dig up any information for you?"

"I'll probably have to do some sort of follow up now that the police have found the paintings. And of course, it's Valentine's Day next week, so there'll have to be something on that." Charley took a final swallow of the tea. She'd been wracking her brain to find an interesting angle for Valentine's Day. She'd considered and dismissed several ideas already. She wanted something fresh and innovative, not the usual fluff of hearts and candy. She expelled a breath of frustration and tucked the problem into the back of her mind so it could stew a while longer. "There is something, though. Do you think Laine can get me a copy of the autopsy on Albert Tyson?"

Since the beginning of the year, Laine Black had resumed her medical training at Kingston General Hospital, although she'd changed her focus from emergency medicine to pathology. A head injury had slowed her physical speech but not how quickly she could process information. The dead, she said, were more patient.

"I thought you were leaving the shooting to Lester," Grace said.

"That's what I thought, too." Lester appeared beside her desk, his pale blue eyes narrowed in consternation.

"Hold on to your hats," Charley said, annoyed. "I am not looking into the shooting specifically. But we do need to find out who was driving the second truck. I don't think the police were able to recover any shell casings in the snow, so we don't know how many shots were fired. And they're being awfully tight-lipped about the bullet, or bullets, they pulled out of the body. I can't help wondering why unless they think it might tell us something about the shooter, and that will point directly back to the second set of thieves."

"Shouldn't you leave that to Spadina? He's the one Senator Overstreet hired to find his wife's artwork," Lester said. "Or maybe he's finished since they've been found."

Finished?

Mark had been hired to find the paintings, not the thieves. Did he consider his job to be done? Was that why he didn't seem interested in anything she'd learned since?

Well, *she* wasn't finished. There were still too many unanswered questions. Had Clarice been having an affair with Tyson? And if so, did it have anything to do with his decision to steal the paintings?

And if Clarice had been involved with Tyson, what did that say about the true nature of her relationship with her husband? Was she drawn to the handyman from loneliness? Or was Mark right and she was nothing more than a gold digger who'd cuckolded the senator?

"I don't know what Mark's doing," Charley said. "But I'm not done. That fellow arrested by the police—Dowden? —did I read they've let him go?"

"Yeah, yesterday afternoon," Lester said. "Since he didn't end up taking the artwork, the Overstreets don't want to press charges for the theft. The cops aren't happy about it, but I guess they figure they've got bigger fish to fry."

"Has Dowden said anything more about what happened? Why they wanted the paintings? What they were going to do with them?"

"Not to my knowledge."

Charley eyed Pyne. Why hadn't he tried to interview the man? Get a scoop for the *Trib* on what had really happened when Tyson was shot Friday morning? The murder was his story.

But she knew the answer. Lester had moved on. Unless or until someone was arrested for Tyson's murder, the story had gone stale. He wasn't interested in looking at the bigger picture. But then, he didn't know everything that Charley did. Whether it ended up in the *Trib* or not, she needed answers and Dowden could give them to her—at least she hoped he could.

The telephone on her desk rang.

Finally!

Grace and Lester wandered back to their desks as she answered. But it was neither Brownie nor Mark.

Dan wanted to see her.

THERE WAS no one in the reception area of Dan's City Hall office when Charley arrived, and his door was slightly ajar.

"Dan?"

"C'mon in, Charley."

"Where's Diana?" She pushed open the door and crossed the room toward the desk where Dan sat. Diana Huff was rarely far from her boss's side as Dan divided his time between his job as a corporate lawyer for his family's shipbuilding company and his elected position of city alderman. Charley enjoyed sparring with the woman. She was over-protective and probably more than a little in love with her boss, but she was also meticulously efficient, and Dan would be lost without her.

"She's at the shipyard. I wasn't supposed to be here today, but I forgot some files I need to go over before Wednesday's council meeting. And once I got here..." He shrugged. "You know how it goes." He pushed his chair back, stood and stretched, his white dress shirt straining across his broad chest.

She looked away, uncomfortably warm by the intimacy of his action, and then chastised herself for being silly. She'd seen Dan in all manner of dress over the years. An unbuttoned collar and rolled-up sleeves shouldn't be enough to set her heart fluttering so.

"Can I get you a coffee? There's probably some in one of the other offices that we can swipe."

"No, I'm fine. Thanks." Charley swallowed heavily and sank into the nearest chair in case her wobbly legs betrayed her. "Why did you want to see me?"

Dan sat in the chair beside her. "I'm sorry I wasn't home when you came by on Friday." Was it her imagination or did he look a little flushed, too?

"That's all right. It was Meredith we needed to talk to."

"Yes, well, ah…"

"And I managed to track her down, despite the fact you hadn't bothered to tell me you'd bought a new home and had moved into it." Charley tried to keep her tone even to soften her pique. She still hadn't forgiven him. And to have found out from Mark, of all people!

"I'm sorry." Dan put his head in his hands. "It was unforgivable of me." He raised his gaze to her. "It happened so quickly and, well, we haven't seen much of each other since the wedding."

"Except at the *vernissage*." She wasn't going to let him off the hook that easily.

"Oh yeah, that." He grinned sheepishly.

"Yeah, that." She steeled herself against the little flip-flop of her heart. "Look, it's fine. You don't—"

"I wanted to apologize for what happened at the *vernissage*, too," he interrupted. "Meredith was a little harsh."

"We were being silly," she said.

"It was innocent fun. We weren't upsetting anyone."

"Except Meredith." Charley could still feel the sting of her rebuke.

He nodded. "But those paintings were pretty awful, weren't they?"

Charley didn't rise to the bait. "Meredith seems to know quite a bit about abstract art," she said instead.

"Art in general. It was part of the curriculum at her fancy Swiss boarding school. Why?"

It had been niggling at her ever since she and Mark had spoken with Jean-Philippe Leloup. "She thought they were good, exceptional even. And yet, when we spoke to the art critic, he dismissed them as drivel."

"Perhaps he isn't a fan of the form," Dan suggested.

"Maybe, but as a critic, I'd expect him to be more open to a variety of styles. I find it odd that two of the best-educated people on the subject had such different reactions to the collection."

"I don't know what to tell you. Meredith loved the paintings, went on and on about how bold and daring they were—especially for a female artist. Hey, maybe that's it. Maybe the critic doesn't like women artists."

"That could be." Mark had made a similar suggestion after their encounter with Leloup. "What did Meredith's brother think? I was surprised to see him there."

"I don't know what he thought. He didn't say. And why wouldn't Colin be there? He's a supporter of the Liberal party and Overstreet is always mixing business with pleasure."

"Did you ever talk to the senator about supporting your bid for the party's nomination in the next election?"

Dan glanced down and straightened the pleat in his trousers. "No, it didn't come up. If I didn't know better, I'd say Overstreet is avoiding me."

"What about Colin? Isn't part of his job to promote your candidacy?"

"Why are you so curious about Colin?"

"Do you know if he lost a cuff link that night?"

"What?" Dan's head shot up and his eyes narrowed.

"Mrs. Rinehart said a man came to the house, after everyone had left, asking to be let in to look for a missing cuff link. She said he had an accent she didn't recognize. I thought it might have been Colin. Not many people around here are familiar with a South African accent."

Dan shook his head. "I have no idea if he lost a cuff link. That's a strange thing to be pursuing. I thought you and Spadina were looking for art thieves."

"We are. I am trying to follow every lead."

"Look, Charley, I know you don't like Colin, but jeepers, you can't seriously think he's a thief."

Charley cocked an eyebrow at him. *Diamonds? Art? Is there much difference?* She didn't say anything, though. There was no point casting aspersions on the character of Dan's brother-in-law without more proof than the nagging in her gut that there was something wrong about him—aside from the fact he'd hidden a fortune in diamonds from the government when he'd emigrated after the war.

"Can I ask you something else?" she said to change the subject. "What do you hear about Senator Overstreet's reputation around Ottawa."

"Is this part of your case, too?" Dan raised an eyebrow.

"There have been rumours of his philandering for years," Charley said. "I was wondering if they've continued now that he's remarried."

"You know I don't go in for gossip." Dan stood.

"But don't you think it's strange that he doesn't take Clarice to Ottawa with him when he's there so much of the time?"

"I don't know if it's strange or not."

"If you're elected, will you leave Meredith here while you go off to sit in Parliament for weeks on end? Charley asked.

"Of course not. But Meredith is eager to be a politician's wife. You don't know if Clarice feels the same way. Maybe it is her decision to remain in Kingston."

Charley leaned back in her chair to consider that. Meredith was not only eager to be a politician's wife, but she'd also been groomed for the role. What experience would Clarice have? Before marrying Overstreet, she'd been a waitress. But surely, the senator could have introduced her to people who would help her. She was young, but she must have had some inkling of what would be expected of her once she married a prominent member of Canada's political system.

So, where does Tyson fit in?

The senator wasn't the only one subject to rumours of infidelity.

"The reason I asked you here," Dan began, interrupting her thoughts.

She glanced up, surprised to find him back behind his desk. "You mean it wasn't to apologize for not telling me you'd moved?"

"Well, that, too," he admitted, wincing at the barb. "But no. The reason was to ask you to come to dinner tomorrow night. Meredith has invited Poppy over before she heads back to Montreal, and we thought it would be fun to get the gang—"

"No!" Charley leapt to her feet as the word shot out of her mouth. Was he kidding? Spend an evening with Dan and the woman who'd stolen him from her in high school as well as the one who'd stolen him in marriage? Horrifying!

"C'mon, Charley. It's been years. Surely long enough for you and Poppy to have buried the hatchet."

"Only if it's in her chest," Charley muttered as she stalked out of the office.

STANLEY DOWDEN LIVED north of Kingston's downtown core. It was a longer walk than Charley might normally have taken, but she was so steamed by Dan and his ludicrous dinner invitation that she felt the physical exertion would benefit her and anyone she encountered that day. Unfortunately, she hadn't counted on the amount of slush in the streets from the melting snow. Why hadn't the city put sidewalks in residential areas like they had downtown? She'd take it up with Dan once she started speaking to him again.

She'd called Dowden's home from a pay phone in the lobby of City Hall. His wife, Barbara, had answered and encouraged Charley to come and stay for lunch. She was anxious to clear her husband's name. Although he hadn't been charged, she didn't feel the newspapers had done enough to assert his innocence after they'd declared him guilty on their front pages. Charley wasn't sure how much she could help with that, but she was determined to get to the bottom of what had happened that morning. If she could, she'd make sure the story got into the *Trib*, even if it were only on the women's pages.

On the street, at the address Barbara Dowden had given

her, a man was scrubbing at the side of a white delivery truck.

"Mr. Dowden?" Charley guessed.

"Mrs. Hall." The man placed the brush he was holding in a bucket of steaming water. After attempting to dry his wet hand on his trousers, he extended it in a greeting.

Charley forced herself to ignore the cold clammy flesh so that she could return his firm handshake. That was one point in his favour. She hated it when men offered limp greetings to women. They probably thought they were being respectful of the "weaker" sex, but she found it insulting and always made certain she let them know their error with a firm grip.

Dowden was younger than she'd expected—not yet thirty, she was sure. He had a pleasant, open face that showed no indication of the ordeal he'd undergone the past few days.

"Is that the truck?" Charley asked. He'd managed to remove most of the black painted letters; only the erroneous LRY remained on one of the side panels. She stepped closer and ran her hand over the back door of the truck. "Was there any damage? Bullet holes, I mean?" She wheeled around when she heard his sharp intake of breath. "Oh, I'm so sorry. That was callous of me."

"It's okay." He uncovered his head exposing a mass of brown hair that stuck out at all angles and rolled the grey woollen toque vigorously between his hands. "That's a fair question. The police went over it pretty thoroughly and didn't find anything." He picked up the bucket. "Let's go inside. Barbara is anxious to meet you. She's a huge fan."

The door swung open as soon as they stepped onto the front porch and two small bodies hurled toward them.

Dowden lowered his bucket to pick up one. Charley managed to grab the second one before it reached the steps.

"Nice catch." Dowden grinned at her as he easily threw the squirming bundle over his shoulder.

Charley stared at the wriggling package in her arms. "Hello," she said. "What's your name?"

It stopped moving and stared up at her with enormous blue eyes. "Ronald Alexander Simon Dowden," he pronounced.

"That's quite a mouthful," Charley said, following Dowden inside where she put the child down.

"And I'm Donald Alistair Stephen Dowden," the second boy proclaimed as his father lowered him to the ground.

"Well, I'm Charlotte Elizabeth Cynthia Stormont Hall. But you can call me Charley."

"No fair!" Donald said. "You've got one more name than us."

"That's because I'm married, so I was given an extra name."

"Oooh." The boys nodded in unison. They looked back at their mother who was accepting the bucket from Dowden. "Did you get an extra name, too, Mommy?"

"I did." Barbara Dowden smiled down at her boys before shifting her gaze to wink at Charley.

"Oh, goodie." Ronald clapped his hands. "I can't wait to get married so I can get another name."

"I want mine to be Humpty Dumpty," Donald said as he danced his way around his mother to the back of the house.

"That's two names," Ronald scolded as he ran after his brother. "I want mine to be Rumpelstiltskin."

"They're adorable," Charley said. "How old are they?"

"Four," Dowden said.

"And we have another son, Mitchell, who's a year old, and is finally down for his nap," Barbara said proudly.

"Three boys. I bet they're a handful," Charley remarked.

"That they are. But considering how many young men we lost in the war, well, I feel proud that we're able to help Canada by doing our part, so to speak. Does that sound foolish?" She flushed slightly as she looked to her husband for support.

"Not at all, dear," Dowden said, kissing her cheek. "Above and beyond, I'd say."

"You went overseas?" Charley asked. It made sense that Dowden had fought in the war, come home and started a family, doing what the government was encouraging all its returning soldiers to do.

"Yeah."

Charley recognized the clipped, one-syllable response. Like so many others she'd encountered, he was tight-lipped about his war experiences. She respected that. After all, it had taken her brother two years to talk about his. "Is there somewhere I can hang my coat and hat?" she asked.

"Oh, how thoughtless of me. Here, I'll take them. And your boots, too. I'll put them by the fire to dry out some." Barbara handed the bucket back to Dowden so she could take Charley's things. "Stan, show her into the kitchen. I've got a potato and mutton soup on the stove and some bread fresh from the baker's this morning."

Charley appreciated the steaming bowl of soup. It was delicious. Once they were all settled at the table, she turned to Dowden and asked him about Albert Tyson.

"I knew him from some jobs we'd done together. He seemed a good bloke," Dowden said.

"Was he from here?"

"No, Hudson," he said and then seeing Charley's confusion, added, "It's in Quebec."

"And you worked together?"

"Sometimes. He is—was—a carpenter. A good one, too. I do a lot of jobs for builders and the like, you know, moving things for them in my truck. So, I'd run into him a lot and we hit it off."

"He was wonderful with the boys," Barbara said.

"It was more than a work friendship?" Charley asked.

"He was all by himself and new to Kingston, so we'd ask him for Sunday dinner," Barbara said.

"Did he have a girlfriend?"

"Not that he ever said, at least not to me." Dowden looked at his wife.

"He never mentioned anyone," Barbara said.

"How long had he been here?" Charley continued.

Dowden shrugged. "A year maybe?"

"Did he say why he left Hudson?" Charley was curious about the timing. How close was Hudson to Montreal?

"Probably for a job. I met him when they were building all those new homes in the west end for the returning vets. There's a lot of work here. He must have been doing pretty well, too, because he started taking on more jobs on his own—at least that's what I figured since I didn't see him at many of the big construction sites very often."

"Did you know he'd done work for the Overstreets?"

"Not until the police mentioned it." Dowden rubbed his chin. "I didn't think much of it at the time, but after, it did occur to me that he did seem to know his way around the place—exactly where to go, park the truck, that sort of thing."

"Can you tell me what happened Friday morning?" Charley asked.

"Sure. He'd telephoned earlier in the week to ask to use the truck for a job he had coming up."

"Did he do that often?"

"Occasionally."

"It wasn't out of the ordinary," Barbara said. "And Fridays aren't usually very busy for Stan, you understand."

"I don't suppose the building contractors want supplies delivered right before a weekend," Charley said. "Go on."

"He came by the night before and insisted we paint the truck to make it look like it came from an art gallery. I wasn't crazy about the idea, but he said it would be worth it once we were paid for the job. We got the sides done before the storm hit. Albert said that was good enough and we needn't bother with the back."

"What about the uniforms? Weren't you concerned that between painting the truck and asking you to wear a fake police uniform that what you were doing might be illegal?"

"Sure, it crossed my mind. He said the uniforms were for show, to make a good impression for the person who hired him. Albert was a good egg. I didn't believe he would do anything crooked."

"And he wouldn't do anything that would hurt Stan and our family," Barbara insisted. "I know what they're saying about him, but I refuse to believe he was evil."

"Okay. Can you take me step-by-step through what happened from the time he arrived Friday morning?" Charley asked.

"Yeah. He arrived before seven. It was snowing something fierce, so it was slow going. I suggested waiting a few hours—at least until it was light out—but Albert said he couldn't wait. I figured he had another job, so I didn't argue.

I was happy to be done and home early." Dowden cut a large slice off the loaf and slathered it with butter. "We pulled up in front of this enormous house and he told me to go up to the front door and let them know we'd come for the crates." He took a bite and chewed thoughtfully. "As soon as I got out of the truck, he slid into the driver's seat and drove over to the wing that juts out on the side. I rang the bell and told the maid what Albert told me to. She pointed over to the wing and said they were in there. I walked back to where Albert had parked the truck and opened up the back and went in to get the crates."

"Did the housekeeper have to unlock the door for you?" Charley asked.

"No, it was already unlocked."

"If Albert stayed in the truck until you came back, then the housekeeper wouldn't have seen him?" Charley had wondered how Albert had managed to escape Mrs. Rinehart's detection during the theft.

"I suppose so."

"And then what happened?"

"We went into the building. There were four large wooden crates stacked up against a wall at the end of the room. We each grabbed one and took it out to the truck. Albert put his in the back and I went to put mine on top, but he stopped me and said they needed to be stacked just so. I was starting to get annoyed with the whole thing, so I left him by the truck to do the stacking and went back inside to get another one. I was inside getting the last one when I heard Albert yelling something. I didn't pay him much attention figuring he was telling me to hurry up—he could be impatient like that." Dowden took a deep breath. "Then there was a popping sound that I knew right away was a gunshot."

"Only one shot?" Charley asked.

"No—more than that. Three maybe?" He shook his head. "I dropped the crate I was holding and ran out. Albert was lying behind the truck not moving. There was so much blood. I knelt beside him and checked his vitals—I sometimes helped the medics during the war—and knew right away he was dead. I looked around and saw the blue truck and some men coming toward me. I figured I needed to get out of there fast."

"Leaving Albert." There was no way to soften the comment.

"I'm no coward, Mrs. Hall. I would never have abandoned my friend if he were still alive. But I have a wife and kids to think about."

"Of course, you do. I wasn't implying you'd done anything dishonourable. I'm trying to understand exactly what happened. Did you get a good look at the men from the blue truck? How many did you see?"

"I don't know how many there were, and I didn't stick around to see what they wanted. I figured they shot Albert so I took off before they could get a bead on me."

"It sounds like it all happened very quickly. You're lucky you got away," Charley said, keeping her tone sympathetic. She was disappointed at how little Dowden remembered about the second set of thieves, but she didn't want him to clam up. She had more questions. "What happened to the crates that were loaded in the back of your truck?"

"I guess they slid out when I drove away. I didn't take the time to close the back door."

"Where did you go when you left?"

"He came here," Barbara said. "We talked about it and decided he needed to call the police."

"*You* called the cops?" That was news to Charley.

"Yeah. I didn't know what else to do. My friend had been murdered and I didn't think I'd done anything wrong."

"You didn't," Barbara said emphatically. "That's why, once they knew all the facts, the police released you."

"When did you place the call?" Charley asked. "Was it as soon as you got home?"

"No." Dowden lowered his head.

"We talked about it a while," Barbara said. "Stan was pretty shaken up when he got here, and it took a bit for the story to come out."

"So how long would you say it was between the time you left the Overstreet home and when you called the police?"

Barbara and Stan looked at each other, considering. Finally, Stan shrugged his shoulders. "Probably forty, forty-five minutes. I know I should have called right away, but..."

"The police had already been alerted. They'd received a call from the Overstreet house, not minutes before Stan called them." Barbara reached across the table and took his hand. "It was all such a shock," she said, giving him a squeeze for support.

Charley could only imagine how much of a shock. When he'd left the house that morning, Dowden had thought he was doing a simple favour for a friend. When he returned, his friend was dead, and he'd been drawn into something nefarious. "Do you know why Albert wanted the paintings?" Charley asked.

"He never said what they were," Dowden replied. "I didn't know they were paintings until the cops told me when they took me in."

"Do you know if Albert had an interest in art?" Charley had hoped Dowden would help shed some light on why Tyson had done it, but she was no closer to learning the truth than she had been when she arrived. If the man was having an affair with Clarice, why would he steal from her? Perhaps Mrs. Rinehart had got it wrong and Tyson wasn't romancing the young bride but was using her to gain access to the home so he could rob it. But why take the paintings when there were so many more valuable objects in the Overstreets' home? And why do it that morning when the house was full of people?

"Tell her what you told me last night," Barbara urged her husband.

Dowden frowned. "I have no proof. It's a hunch, that's all."

"Some of my best stories come from hunches," Charley prompted.

"Well, I'm pretty sure taking the paintings wasn't Albert's idea. He kept talking about a big payday. And I can't remember exactly what he said, but I got the impression he was working for a dame."

"Doesn't look like anyone is here." Romeo Arcadi raised his gaze to meet Charley's in the rear-view mirror of his taxi.

She'd called the cabbie to pick her up from the Dowdens' so she could avoid slogging through the mushy slush again.

A dame.

Clarice?

She'd told Charley she hadn't wanted to exhibit her artwork. Her husband had gone against her wishes. Had Clarice arranged for her lover to "steal" the collection? If so, things had gone tragically wrong when the thieves from the blue truck arrived. Perhaps it was Tyson's murder more than the loss of the paintings that explained her distress. If Charley was honest with herself, she had to agree with Mark's assertion that it seemed excessive.

She turned her head to look through the storefront window into Mark's darkened office. Arcadi was right. It didn't look like he was in.

"I'll try the door to be sure," she said.

With all that she'd learned since they'd found the burned-out second delivery van on the weekend, she decided she could swallow her pride—in the best interest of the case—and reach out to Mark to get his impression of what it could all mean.

She rattled the door handle. Locked. She pounded on the black wooden door anyway, more out of frustration than any expectation of a response. Blowing out her annoyance, she scowled at the brass nameplate Gran had given him for Christmas. *Spadina Private Detective Agency.* He'd seemed genuinely pleased, announcing it would raise his cachet and possibly attract a better calibre of client.

"You can't have clients if you're never here," she grumbled returning to the cab.

"Where to now?" Arcadi asked.

Mark's favourite eatery, Joe's Diner, was around the corner. He might be there. And if not, Gillian, the waitress, may know where he'd gone or when he was coming back.

Has it come to this?

Hunting him down like a jealous wife?

It wasn't the first time he'd disappeared on her in the middle of a case. Despite his declaration that they were a team, he liked to keep her in the dark much of the time. She cringed at how pleased she'd been that he'd included her in his investigation into the theft. She should have known better.

Mark did what was best for Mark. What he'd needed was intimate access to the Overstreet family and its secrets—something Charley could give him. At the time.

Now?

Well, now he had Poppy, didn't he?

Maybe Lester was right and Mark did consider his job done now that the police had discovered the burned canvases. But for Charley, this wasn't any old case. Too many questions had been raised about people she'd once considered family. Whether or not she liked the answers, she was going to follow the story through to the end.

"Take me to Senator Overstreet's home, please."

"It's almost like old times with you showing up every day," Mrs. Rinehart said, taking Charley's coat and hat.

Charley sat down on the bench to remove her boots and slip her chilled feet into a warm pair of knitted slippers. "Is that a problem?"

"Of course not. You've always been welcome here."

Charley stood and gave the housekeeper a cynical smile. "Not by everyone."

"Well, girls will be girls, won't they? I was always sorry you and Poppy fell out." She tucked a wayward strand of Charley's hair behind her ears in a familiar gesture that caused Charley's breath to catch. "Now, are you here to see Mrs. Overstreet or the senator? I am quite certain it isn't Poppy."

"I was hoping to speak with Mrs. Overstreet. But first, I have something I want to show you." Charley reached into her pocketbook and took out a news clipping. She unfolded the paper. "This is a picture taken at Dan Cannon's wedding. I am wondering if this man, beside the bride, could be the 'foreigner' who came to the house Thursday night."

"I recognize him. His picture has been in the newspaper quite a bit, hasn't it? This is the fellow you mentioned the other day?"

"Yes. That's Colin Banks."

Mrs. Rinehart returned the newspaper to her. "I'm quite certain I've never seen him in person."

"So not the mysterious visitor," Charley said, disappointed.

"Oh no. That gentleman was quite the opposite of your Mr. Banks. He was very tall and slim—skinny, even. What I remember most, though, was he had bushy black eyebrows."

"Bushy black eyebrows," Charley repeated. Why hadn't she said that before? "Oh well, back to the drawing board." She folded and returned the clipping to her pocketbook. "Have you given more thought to telling the police about him?"

"Oh no. I wouldn't even broach the subject with the senator. I'm sure if he decides it's important, he'll go to the police himself. Now, make yourself comfortable and I'll see if Mrs. Overstreet will see you."

Charley glanced toward the hallway leading to the east wing. She'd love to take another look in there but didn't feel she could chance it. Besides, it was Clarice's locked studio she wanted to get into. Perhaps she could convince the woman to give her a tour.

She wandered down the hallway to the back of the house, intending to wait in the conservatory. As she approached, she noticed the door to the senator's office was ajar and she veered toward it.

Overstreet was sitting behind his desk, his elbows on its surface and his forehead resting on his hands.

"Senator?" Charley hesitated in the doorway.

Overstreet raised his head with a start and Charley took a chance and approached his desk. He looked terrible. His eyes were red and swollen and his skin was a sallow grey. He hadn't shaved in several days.

"Is there something I can do for you?" she asked.

He sighed and shook his head. "I wish there was,

Charley, but no, I'm afraid I've botched things up and I don't know how to make it right."

"Is it Clarice?"

He nodded and rubbed his bandaged hand. "Yes. I don't know if she'll ever forgive me."

"Because you insisted on an exhibition of her paintings?"

"She told you, did she?" He sighed. "I know she's been struggling with her role as a senator's wife. I thought if I showed an interest in something so important to her that it would prove how much I love her. She wouldn't need any —" He gulped as a shudder wracked his body. "I thought I would be enough."

"But she said she didn't want to show them."

"I thought she was being modest."

"And now the paintings are gone. Does she blame you?"

"Who else is responsible?"

"The thieves who stole them," Charley said. "You couldn't have possibly known that would happen."

"No, but there's no doubt that my insistence on a public exhibition put it all in motion."

"Can you go over again what happened Friday morning?"

Overstreet sighed heavily. "I've explained it so many times before, I don't know what difference it will make."

"Humour me, please."

"All right. Clarice and Poppy slept through the whole thing. I awoke at six, as usual. I came to my office where Mrs. Rinehart had a thermos of hot coffee waiting. I wrote in my journal—random thoughts about my life, the state of the world...that sort of thing." He looked down, embarrassed. "I hope to publish it someday. There might be a nugget or two that the younger generation would benefit from."

"I am sure there's a whole mine full of golden nuggets."

"Do you think so? Would you like to read it?" He looked at her hopefully.

Charley shifted uncomfortably in her chair. "I'm not an editor, so I don't think I'd be in the best position to help you with it. But I can make inquiries and see who has experience editing memoirs if you like."

Overstreet nodded thoughtfully. "That would be most appreciated."

"You were in your study..." Charley encouraged him to continue.

"Ah, yes. I went for my morning constitutional—"

"Even in the snowstorm?"

"Never miss it. As soon as the sun's up, I take a brisk hour-long walk along the lake. It helps clear out the cobwebs and makes for a more productive day. But that morning was a shorter walk than usual. After fifteen minutes, I decided to return home."

"What happened when you got back?"

"Usually Clarice is up by then and we have breakfast together. But as I said, I returned much earlier than usual. Neither she nor Poppy was awake, so I went back to my study."

"And that was where Mrs. Rinehart found you and told you about the shooting and the theft."

Overstreet shrugged. "More or less."

"What do you mean?"

"Do you need this much detail, Charley? That's essentially all of it."

"It's a hazard of my job, I'm afraid. What happened when you got back to your study?"

"I can see why you're such a good reporter." He leaned back and closed his eyes as if he was trying to replay in his mind the events of that morning. "All right." He looked at her. "Shortly after I got back, Mrs. Rinehart came in and apologized profusely for not having breakfast ready. She seemed quite distressed—well, you know how efficient she is. I told her there was no reason to expect a change in the usual breakfast time and returned to work. A while later she came back in a real tizzy, saying she'd heard a commotion in the east wing and felt I should go investigate."

"Did she say what kind of commotion? Did she mention the shooting?"

"No, she wasn't specific. But Mrs. Rinehart has worked for us long enough that if she says there is something I need to attend to, I don't question her."

"So, you went to the east wing," she prompted.

"Yes. I didn't see anything untoward, except perhaps that the men collecting the paintings had left puddles of water and slush from their boots. The door was closed, and the paintings were gone. I went to lock the door. I don't know what made me open it first, but when I did, I saw that man lying bloody in the snow, not five feet away."

"And both trucks were gone?"

"Yes. After I made certain he was dead, I told Mrs. Rinehart to call the police and that's it. Does that satisfy you, Reporter Hall?"

"Yes, thank you, Senator," Charley said, although there was still something niggling in the back of her mind. She couldn't quite get at it, so she decided to pursue a different path. "Can I ask you something else?" She waited for him to nod his assent. "Why didn't you take Clarice to Ottawa with you?"

A flush crept up Overstreet's cheeks and Charley

wondered if she'd overstepped. Gran would be horrified that she'd asked such a personal question of her elder.

"I asked her to join me. Every time I left I'd beg her to come with me. At first, she said she felt inadequate and wasn't sure she knew how to fit in and behave. She asked for more time to become accustomed to her role. Then later... well, she had her painting."

"It was her decision not to go?"

Overstreet's eyes creased at the corners as his mouth pulled up into a sad imitation of a smile. "No doubt you've heard the rumours. Well, they're true. Or I should say, they used to be." He picked at a loose thread from the linen bandage on his hand. "This isn't the type of thing a man of my age discusses with a young woman, let alone a friend of his daughter's, and especially not a reporter. But I trust you, Charley. You know us. Our history. And frankly, I don't know who else to talk to about this."

"I was young, but I was aware that your relationship with your first wife wasn't a particularly close one."

"Very tactful. Bessie's taught you well." The senator chuckled darkly. "My first marriage was arranged to benefit my family socially and Henrietta's family financially. We never loved each other, didn't like each other much if I'm being honest. But we managed to make it work—mostly by living separate lives and coming together when it was required. I was so hopeful things would be different with Clarice. I wanted to share every part of my life with her."

"You love her." Charley didn't phrase it as a question. It was obvious from the look on his face that he was completely smitten with his new bride and totally baffled by what to do about it.

"Just like one would read in those trashy romance novels Henrietta used to read."

"Does she feel the same way about you?"

"I wish I knew. I thought she did when she agreed to marry me. Our courtship and honeymoon were magical. But once we returned here and I had to get back to work, everything seemed to change. It was as if she'd lost confidence in herself. She claimed she wouldn't know the proper things to do or say if she went to Ottawa with me. I told her some of the wives of close political friends would be more than happy to take her under their wings to teach her, but she refused. And yet, when we entertain here, she handles it all so effortlessly—as if she were born to it. She could show some of those Ottawa wives a thing or two about grace and style."

"Oh, here you are." Mrs. Rinehart pushed the office door open wide. "I'm afraid Mrs. Overstreet is not up to receiving visitors at the moment," she said to Charley. "And Senator it's almost time for your five o'clock telephone call with the caucus whip."

Charley rose and followed the housekeeper to the foyer. As she walked the few blocks to her home in the dimming light of the late afternoon, she felt completely turned upside-down.

Overstreet had seemed desperate in his desire to do whatever he could to please his young wife. But Clarice claimed she turned to painting as a refuge because her husband left her alone so much of the time.

The senator had the reputation for extramarital affairs and yet Clarice was supposedly the unfaithful one.

Topsy-turvy. Inside-out.

And it got her no closer to figuring out if Clarice was in on the original heist, who the thieves in the blue truck were, and why Tyson was murdered over four paintings by an unknown artist.

"I AM SO glad you changed your mind," Meredith whispered as she embraced Charley affectionately. "I think you know everyone here."

Charley glanced around the drawing room of the Cannons' new home. She'd expected only Poppy. The opportunity for an intimate conversation with her former best friend was the reason she'd come—yes, she was that desperate to understand what was happening with the Overstreet family. But there was Mark, sitting comfortably beside her on the sofa. He rose as Charley entered the room and took a step toward her. She turned away, still miffed at how easily he'd abandoned her and their investigation. By the fireplace, Dan was talking to another man. As recognition hit, she called out his name with real pleasure, "Hal!" and hurried across the room.

The man embraced her, kissed her on the cheek, and then took a step back and gazed at her appreciatively. "Look at you, Charley. How long has it been?"

"Too long. When did you get to town?" Charley was undertaking her own examination. Hal Overstreet, the senator's son from his first marriage, was the spitting image of his father. Tall and broad-shouldered, with a curly mass of sandy blond hair, a neatly trimmed beard, and kind brown eyes. Four years older than Charley and Poppy, he'd often been called upon to babysit when Mrs. Rinehart had to run errands. He never seemed to mind, and Charley had many fond memories of scavenger hunts and games of hide-and-seek where no room was out of bounds. She'd heard that he'd joined the Canadian diplomatic corps after the war and had been posted to Chicago when the new consulate was established in 1947.

"I arrived this afternoon. I was caught in that storm and had a heck of a time getting out of Chicago. I am sorry I wasn't here when all the trouble happened with Clarice's paintings and that fellow who was killed."

"I am sure your father and Clarice are happy you're here now. And Poppy, of course," she added hastily.

Hal chuckled, fully aware of the tension between Charley and his sister but completely unaffected by it. "I was very sorry to hear about Theo," he said, his eyes softening as his expression became serious. "He was a swell guy. I was his squad leader in outdoor club and man, did he keep me on my toes. He and Freddie."

"Thank you. Yes, we all miss Theo. His death is a terrible loss to us all."

"How is your brother, by the way? He must have taken it pretty hard. They were so close. I heard he was there. The landing at Dieppe, right?"

Charley swallowed the lump that seemed to lodge in her throat every time she thought about how close she'd come to losing her brother, too. "Freddie struggled when he first came home, but he seems to be doing much better."

"Glad to hear it. Hey, can I get you a drink?" He glanced to the sideboard, beside the room's entrance, where an assortment of beverages was laid out. "Champagne for the lady? Or maybe since you're now a hard-nosed reporter, it's whiskey." He raised his eyebrows pretending to be scandalized by the thought.

"Only a small sherry before dinner, please," she responded, mimicking Gran's best imperial tone.

"Of course, forgive my blunder, madam." He bowed deeply. "I'll be back in a jiffy."

Charley grinned and shook her head at their tomfoolery. It had been a long time since she'd felt this light-hearted. There was an ease to Hal that she admired. He'd maneuvered through the difficult task of offering his condolences to brightening her mood without making it seem forced.

"What the heck?" Dan said from behind her.

She whirled around to see his brows knitted together and a deep frown on his face. He was as pale as a ghost, which made sense considering what he'd just heard. Mark had joined him, but he didn't look as perturbed. "What?" she asked.

"You snap your cap any time someone even suggests that Theo might be dead—" he sputtered.

"Ease up, Sport," Mark interrupted him. "Freddie was finally able to talk about what happened to Theo."

Charley swallowed past the lump that had lodged in her throat.

Mark knows.

Why hadn't he said anything about it? Was he waiting for her to admit it so he could tell her "I told you so"?

"When was this?" Dan asked.

"Christmas Eve," Charley said, turning from Mark to Dan.

Dan's eyes widened and he took a step back as if she'd punched him in the gut. He'd married Meredith on Christmas Eve—went ahead with the wedding because Charley had refused his numerous proposals, always on the basis that she had no proof Theo was dead and she'd promised to wait for him.

"It makes no difference," Charley said raising her chin defiantly.

"Are you so sure about that?" Dan choked out before he spun on his heel and stalked off to join his wife who had taken a seat beside Poppy.

She glanced up at Mark, but there was no look of triumph in his dark eyes, only compassion. "Excuse me," she said, making her own quick escape. Tenderness from Mark wasn't something she knew what to do with.

Meredith was the perfect hostess, of course, although Charley did catch her giving Dan the evil eye when her attempts to have him join the conversation flopped. Poppy had affixed herself to Mark's side and he didn't seem to mind in the least. The evening was made bearable solely thanks to Hal, who regaled them with witty stories about his posting in Chicago.

When it was time to leave, Mark offered to drive the three guests home. At first, Charley resisted, insisting she could walk but that caused so much consternation she finally gave in.

As Mark turned into the Overstreets' driveway—the logical first stop—Charley could hear the irritation in Poppy's voice as she first criticized his chosen route and then pestered him to, at least, return for a nightcap.

"How long are you going to be in town?" Charley asked Hal, sitting beside her in the backseat so she wouldn't have to hear Mark's response.

"I'm not sure. I'm considering returning to Canada permanently. What would you think about that?"

"I think it would be wonderful," Charley said.

Hal took her hand and squeezed it gently. "I am glad to hear it."

Too late, Charley feared she might have given him the wrong idea. But then again, he was a well-educated, handsome man with good career prospects. Besides, it wouldn't be long before Gran's friends started finding excuses to introduce Charley to their eligible grandsons. At least she knew Hal and had always liked him. She smiled up at him, feeling a rush of heat as his warm brown eyes gazed back at her. She could do worse.

"Come up into the front," Mark said after Poppy and Hal had exited his sedan.

"Seriously? It's only a couple of blocks."

"I'm not a chauffeur."

"Fine." Charley got out of the backseat and slid in beside him.

Mark put the car in gear and pulled out onto King Street, but instead of turning left toward her home, he turned right to head east and the downtown.

"Where are you taking me?"

"Somewhere warm where we can grab a coffee and talk."

"It's late. I want to go home."

"Too bad."

"What do we have to talk about?" she asked.

He shot her a look, his eyebrows arched in disbelief, but he didn't respond. A few minutes later, he pulled to a stop in front of Joe's Diner.

Inside, she removed her coat and hung it over the back of her chair and put her hat on one of the empty seats. She and Mark were the only customers—but then it was close to midnight in the middle of the week. Most industrious Kingstonians would be home in bed by now.

"You look nice, by the way," Mark said after Gillian had poured their coffees.

Charley looked down at her moss-green cocktail dress. It had a modest high-cut neck collar with three-quarter sleeves and shirring that emphasized her waist before falling into a flowing skirt that stopped just below her knees. It was a big change from her usual pleated trousers and a loose blouse. "Thank you."

He nodded and took a sip of his coffee. He looked rather good himself, she thought. Given how easily he wore formal clothes, no one would imagine he hadn't been born to money, and she couldn't help wondering if he'd rented the dinner jacket or had finally gotten around to buying one.

"Hal seems a good egg," Mark said.

"Yeah. Hard to believe he's Poppy's brother."

Mark snorted. "Careful, Tiger, your claws are showing."

"Can we stop the small talk? Why are we here? And to be clear, if it's so you can say 'I told you so' about Theo, I'm not in the mood."

"Theo?" He stared at her appalled. "I'm glad Freddie was finally able to tell you what happened on that beach, but I could never take pleasure from your pain."

"If it's not that, what is it?"

"The case, of course. What has gotten into you tonight? You're wound up tighter than a drum."

Charley rubbed at the throbbing spot between her eyes. "I'm sorry. I thought you'd finished with the case."

"Because the cops found the paintings? That's only part of it."

"That's the part you were hired for."

"That's true," Mark said, leaning back in his chair. "But that's not the part you're interested in. We're a team. I'm not done until you are."

"If we're such a team, why did you blow me off on Sunday? And where have you been for the past few days?"

"Missed me?" he teased.

She threw him a stern look.

"Okay, okay." He raised his hands in surrender. "I was heading out to catch a train to Ottawa when you called on Sunday. And that's where I've been until this afternoon. I've been looking into the senator, interviewing colleagues, employees, mistresses, anyone I could find."

"Learn anything interesting?"

"I know you want to believe Clarice, but everyone I spoke to told the same story. Harold Overstreet is like a new man since his marriage. There's no indication he's been unfaithful to his wife, and his Ottawa housekeeper says he spends more time in Kingston now than she ever remembers him doing before. He's only in Ottawa as much as he needs to be. I'm sorry, Tiger, but I think he's on the up-and-up."

"Believe it or not, I am relieved to hear it. Although I hate the thought that Clarice was able to pull the wool over my eyes, it broke my heart to think that the senator could be a callous louse. You're not the only one with new information." Charley repeated what Mrs. Rinehart had told her about the strange visit from a "foreigner" and Clarice's affair, as well as Dowden's hunch that Tyson was working for a woman.

"You've been a busy bee, haven't you?" Mark sounded impressed. "So where does this leave us?"

"I think Clarice set up the first theft. She didn't want her paintings shown and she had Tyson steal them."

"That's a nice, neat explanation. But it still leaves us with the second band of thieves. I checked with Marillo when I got back into town and the cops have gotten nothing off the blue truck they found. The license plate was stolen from a car in Sydenham the day before. And they can't trace where the truck came from."

"And the paintings?"

"Given the amount of ash and bits of canvas and wood left, they're pretty sure it was the whole collection that was in that fire."

"So, did the thieves intend to destroy the paintings from the beginning, or were they forced to do it after their truck crashed?"

"I think it was planned," Mark said. "They were picked up by someone. They could easily have taken a painting or two with them if they'd wanted to."

"That eliminates Rothko as a suspect. If there are no paintings, he can't make any money." As she tried to work out various scenarios in her head, she tapped her spoon against her coffee cup until Mark reached out to stop her. His touch startled her, and she dropped the spoon. "It's been bothering me that Leloup said the paintings were rubbish, but Meredith thought they were brilliant."

"It would help if we could narrow down a motive," Mark agreed. "Leloup checked out of his hotel as soon as the busses returned to service Saturday afternoon. I assume he's back in Montreal."

"I don't know if he could tell us anything new. He made his view crystal clear. I do wonder, though, if we could get a list from Rothko of who else he sent bulletins to."

"That's a great idea. We could use another opinion."

"I'll call him in the morning." Charley yawned.

"Okay, I get the hint. I'll take you home." He stood and held out her coat.

"What are you going to do tomorrow?" she asked slipping her arms into the sleeves.

"Poppy's invited me to lunch."

Of course, she has.

"Valentine's Day."

Charley glanced up from her sleek, red, portable Smith-Corona typewriter she preferred to the *Tribune*'s bulky Underwoods. "What about it?"

John Sherman sagged, his small body seeming to deflate as if he knew she was going to disappoint him. "The advertisers want to know what you're doing about it."

"I haven't decided yet," she said, meeting his expectation.

"Cutting it close, aren't you? Valentine's Day is Monday, so we need something for *this* weekend's women's pages. Today is Wednesday."

"I know what day it is," she snapped. "I still have three days to figure something out."

"The advertisers aren't going to be happy."

"That's not my problem. I'm editorial." She turned back to her keyboard and started typing fast as if to emphasize her point. After Sherman had marched back to his office, she glanced down at what she'd written. *Gobbledygook*. She yanked the paper out from the machine, fed a clean sheet into the roller and started again, this time making sure her fingers were on the correct keys.

It was a notice about an upcoming presentation to engineering students at Queen's University, something Charley wouldn't normally bother to include. But Elsie MacGill was an exception. The first female aeronautical engineer and aircraft designer, she'd overseen the production of fighter planes during the war, earning the nickname "Queen of the Hurricanes," and was currently heading a United Nations committee—the first woman to do so—as well as maintaining a private consulting practice in Toronto. Women had been allowed into the Queen's Faculty of Applied Science since 1942, but the numbers were still low. The session was going to be open to the public and Charley hoped Mrs. MacGill would inspire more women to study the sciences.

"Can you come with me?" Grace whispered into her ear.

Charley was surprised to see the *Trib*'s archivist wearing her winter coat and hat. Her pocketbook swung from one hand and a brown-paper wrapped package was clutched in her other. "Are you on your way in?" She glanced at her watch. *Nine forty-five.* It was unlike Grace to be late for work. "Or are you on your way out?"

"I had to pick up a parcel from the train station. Come, I'll make us some tea. You're going to want to see this."

Charley typed the last few sentences and then pulled the notice out of her typewriter, dropping it into the wire basket for the copy editor on her way to the morgue, the name the reporters had given the paper's archive.

Grace had hung up her coat and was filling the electric tea kettle with water from the small sink in the corner. "It's plain old Red Rose, I'm afraid," she said, glancing over her shoulder.

"That's fine." Charley quite liked Red Rose's blend of orange pekoe tea. The biggest advantage was its consistency from one bag to another. Unfortunately, that couldn't be said of all the teas her friend liked to experiment with.

She walked to the high-top table where Grace had put the brown-paper packet. She reached out, about to pick it up when Grace's voice rang out from across the room, "Don't even think about it. You'll spoil my surprise."

"Please tell me you're not going to make me wait for the kettle to boil and the tea to steep," Charley pleaded.

"You are always so impatient." Grace chuckled, coming to the table. She moved the package closer to herself and urged Charley to take one of the high stools before climbing onto her own.

Grace picked up last weekend's newspaper and Charley was surprised to see Lee Rothko's bulletin advertising the *Rouge et Jaune* collection flutter out. "That's where that went. I thought I'd lost it."

"I took it off your desk the other day. I've been looking into it for you." Grace opened the newspaper to the women's pages and laid the bulletin down next to Brownie's photographs from the *vernissage*. "I contacted a couple of newspapers in both Montreal and Toronto and asked them if they knew anything about Mrs. Overstreet or her paintings. No luck in Toronto."

"Not surprising," Charley said. "What about Montreal? That's supposedly the centre of Abstract Expressionism in Canada."

"Yes, it is. And I spoke to a reporter there who has an interest in it. I sent him a copy of the article you wrote and a photo of one of the paintings over the wire. It reminded him of another article he'd seen recently, but because our pictures were black and white, he couldn't be positive. So, he sent me the magazine with the article, which includes full-colour photographs." She handed Charley the packet. "Do you want to do the honours?"

Charley slid her finger under the tape that held the package closed. "What are we looking for, exactly?" Judging by the title, *Le nouvel art du Québec*, it was a French-language art magazine.

"I'm not sure," Grace admitted. "Page thirty-three, he said."

Charley flipped to the page which was dominated by a black and white photograph of the face of a haunted young man with hollowed-out cheeks and sharp, dark features. *Joseph Dotremont défie la spontanéité sur la scène artistique expérimentale québécoise.* "Joseph Dotremont challenges spontaneity in Quebec's experimental art scene," Charley translated. "Or something to that effect."

She lowered the magazine to the tabletop so Grace could look at it, too, and turned the page, gasping at the images that appeared. Her gaze met Grace's and she was relieved to see the archivist looked equally surprised. She turned more pages, counting the photographs. "Four and four," Charley said.

Grace placed the colour bulletin beside its matching pair in the magazine. "That's remarkable."

Charley jumped off her stool and raced back to her desk, grabbing her pocketbook from the bottom drawer. She was pulling Brownie's photographs out of their envelope as she returned to the morgue. She quickly discarded the ones with people and laid out a photo of each of Clarice's paintings.

Grace had taken out a magnifying glass and was comparing the bulletin with one of the paintings in the magazine. "Stroke for stroke," she said, handing the eyepiece to Charley.

"How is this possible?" Charley took another photo and found a matching pair of images in the magazine. Grace was right. The bold strokes were virtually identical among the three paintings. The only difference was their colours. Each painting matched one in each of the other two sets. "Look, even the patterns where the colours blend to form a third colour..." It was astoundingly precise.

"*La collection bleu et rouge* and *bleu et jaune*?" Grace asked, her French accent not much better than Charley's.

Charley scanned the text for the article. "Close." She looked up at her friend. "*La série bleu et rouge* and *La série jaune et bleu.*"

"Does the article say this Joseph Dotremont painted them?"

Charley expelled a breath of frustration. "I only have basic high school French, so I can't get all the nuances, but it looks like Dotremont is from...Wallonia?" She glanced up.

"That's a region in the southern part of Belgium," Grace said.

"He's now living in Montreal, and yes, it seems he is the artist." Charley sighed. "I don't get it." She turned to the next page and watched as Grace matched up Brownie's photographs with another pair of images, and then again on the final spread.

"That's all of them," Grace said.

Charley went back to the beginning of the article to try to glean as much information as she could. "He's from Wallonia but went to Brussels to study art when he was sixteen. He started as a traditional painter but transitioned from realism to abstract about fifteen years ago. And since the war, he's been exploring more expressive forms of art." She scanned the article, but it became quite technical, referencing many artists she'd never heard of. "He arrived at the

Port of Montreal in 1947 and has been working in various commercial enterprises while continuing to explore new frontiers for his art." She searched for a reference to *Les Automatistes* and found it, only to be frustrated that her ability to read French wasn't strong enough to know whether Dotremont was influencing or was influenced by the Quebec art dissidents.

But it was what she read at the very end that almost knocked Charley off her stool. She didn't need to be fluent in French to understand that the article had been written by none other than the art critic Jean-Philippe Leloup.

CHARLEY LIFTED the large brass knocker and rapped it three times against the front door of the Overstreets' home.

"Charley, Mrs. Hall." Mrs. Rinehart stepped back from the door to let her in. "Are you joining us for lunch?"

"No, thank you. I don't have an invitation. I am here to see Mrs. Overstreet."

Mrs. Rinehart's frown was accented by the brighter than usual red lipstick she was wearing today. "She hasn't come down yet. I'm not—"

"I insist." Charley wasn't going to be put off again. "You can tell her I'm here about a friend of hers from Montreal. A Monsieur Dotremont."

"Well, yes, I can ask her, at least. Let me hang up your coat."

Charley opened her satchel while Mrs. Rinehart took her coat and scarf. When she returned, she handed the housekeeper the art magazine already folded open to page thirty-three. "First, though, do you recognize this man?"

"That's him!" she said after barely taking a glance at the photograph. "That's the man who came to the house late Thursday night."

"You're certain?"

Mrs. Rinehart handed her back the magazine. "Yes, quite. Who is he?"

"Another artist." Charley put the magazine away and sat down on the bench to unlace her boots.

"I suppose it's a relief to know he wasn't a thief planning to rob us. I'll go see if Mrs. Overstreet will receive you. Poppy and Detective Spadina are in the conservatory if you'd like to join them."

Not a chance! No, she'd sit right here and wait for Mrs. Rinehart to return.

Charley leaned back, resting her head against the wall, and tried to order her whirling thoughts.

She'd been puzzling over the relationship between Clarice Overstreet and Joseph Dotremont during her walk over from the *Trib*. According to the article, Clarice would still have been in Montreal when Joseph Dotremont arrived from Belgium. Had she met him? Seen his paintings and tried to imitate them?

That didn't make sense. The brush strokes and colour patterns were virtually identical in all three series. One couldn't have been created unless the painter was in the presence of at least one of the others.

But which came first? The *rouge et jaune*, the *bleu et rouge*, or the *jaune et bleu*? And who was the real artist?

She sat up abruptly as another thought occurred to her. Had Clarice and Dotremont painted them together?

She needed to see Clarice to get some answers. Right now, the one thing she knew for certain was that Jean-Philippe Leloup had lied to her. In his article, he'd been ebullient in his praise of Dotremont's work and yet, he'd told them Clarice's paintings were amateurish and a poor imitation of *Les Automatistes*.

She caught sight of movement at the far end of the hallway and stood, expecting to see Mrs. Rinehart coming toward her. But it wasn't the housekeeper. Charley watched Mark slink from the direction of the conservatory and then turn sharply to disappear down the hall that led to the east wing.

What is he up to?

Charley made her way toward the turnoff to the east wing. Keeping her distance, she watched him test the door to the wing, and realizing it was locked, reach up to get the key as she had shown him. He unlocked the door, returned the key and slipped inside.

Glancing behind to make certain she was alone, Charley approached the door. Of course, Mark had locked it after himself, so she repeated his actions, unlocking the door and stepping inside the former playroom.

Mark glared at her from across the room. "What are you doing here?"

"I could ask you the same question," she said, approaching him. "Aren't you supposed to be with Poppy?"

He made a growling sound she took as irritation. "She's on a telephone call with her husband and kids." He turned away and knelt in front of the door to Clarice's art studio.

Charley wondered if his annoyance was due to her unexpected arrival or the intrusion of Poppy's family into their time together. She had reminded him the woman was married—multiple times.

Charley watched over his shoulder as he inserted a long, narrow piece of metal into the keyhole of the door. "You're breaking in?"

"Shhh!" He toyed with the pick and then gently turned the doorknob. He rose, keeping his hand on the knob but not opening the door. "Admit it, Tiger, you've been dying to see inside here, too."

Did he have to look so smug? "Well, sure," she conceded, "but I didn't know picking locks was one of the skills they teach cops."

"Purely self-taught. Stick around, Tiger, I have a lot of skills you don't know about." He wiggled his eyebrows suggestively.

Oh boy! She was sure she was blushing and hated him for being able to fluster her so easily. "Can you just open the door, please?"

"Anything for you, my dear." He executed a sweeping bow as he pushed open the door.

Charley peered into the room, her eyes widening in shock as her brain slowly caught up to what she was seeing.

Mark let out a long whistle of surprise. "I wasn't expecting this," he said, nudging her forward.

The wide, windowless room was luxuriously furnished if one was in the market for a lady's boudoir. But an art studio, this was not. The unadorned walls were painted a creamy rose colour. There was a blush-coloured *chaise-longue* with a discarded blanket along one wall. Beside it was a low wooden table with an open book and a stemmed glass with the remains of some red wine in it. An empty bottle sat on the floor, along with a second, unused glass. There must have been a dozen or more pillows of various sizes, all in shades of pastel pink, scattered around. But it was an enormous bed that dominated the room.

"I've never seen anything like it," Charley said.

"Oh, I have," Mark replied. "But never in a family home."

"Hey! What's going...huh? What the heck?"

Charley turned slowly but couldn't meet Hal's gaze. She could only imagine what he was thinking.

"I thought..." Hal began. "I don't understand."

"That's the understatement of the year," Mark said.

"She said it was an art studio," Hal said, scratching his head. "How did you get in here?"

"Detective Marillo said your stepmother resisted any attempt to search her art studio. The cops weren't happy, but since the room wasn't part of the crime scene, they didn't press the matter," Mark said, ignoring the question. "It's not uncommon for a victim of a crime to be uncooperative, but in this case, it made no sense that she wouldn't want to do whatever she could to help recover her paintings. I think a little pressure would have been warranted."

"It's obvious she wasn't painting in here. But if not that, what was she doing?" Hal paled and seemed a little unsteady on his feet, his gaze focused on the bed.

Charley took his arm and led him out of the room. "Were you looking for us?"

"You," he said, seeming relieved to be away from the room that still held many secrets. "Mrs. Rinehart said you were here, and I wanted to ask you to stay for lunch."

Ever since Mark had opened the door, Charley's stomach felt as if it had dropped through the floor. She suspected eating was the last thing any of them would be interested in doing once news of Clarice's studio was out. She glanced at Mark who was calmly closing the door. Except him. He didn't seem to be fazed at all by the discovery.

"I am going to have to ask the two of you to leave." Hal squared his shoulders and raised his head, taking charge. "This is a personal matter. Family only. I'm sure you understand."

"I'm afraid not," Charley said. "There's more I need to ask Clarice about."

"Jeez, Charley, how much more can there be?" Hal's eyes rounded in panic.

"Enough that the senator is going to want us to stick around."

"You had no right!"

Senator Overstreet turned away from the doorway into the so-called art studio. "This is my home. I have every right."

Charley shifted her weight from foot to foot, discomforted by the rising tension in the room. What should have been a private moment had become very public, witnessed by not only her and Mark but also the senator's children, Hal and Poppy.

Clarice shrank back as Overstreet stalked towards her. "I'd like everyone to leave. Clarice and I need some privacy," he said waving them out.

"Detective Spadina and I should stay," Charley said, moving to stand beside Clarice. "I have some information both of you should hear."

Overstreet turned to Mark. "Why are you still involved? The paintings have been found."

"That's true, but the case hasn't been solved," Mark said.

"I don't care. I only hired you to find the darn things."

"Yes, sir, but I do think it would be to your benefit to give Charley and me some of your time."

"Fine," Overstreet barked in a tone that suggested it was anything but. "Come to my office. But only the two of you."

"But Daddy—" Poppy began.

Overstreet ignored her and took Clarice by the elbow to usher the sobbing woman from the room.

"I hope you've got something good," Mark whispered to Charley as they followed.

"Let's just say that while I wasn't expecting what we found, I wasn't too surprised that it wasn't an art studio."

Mrs. Rinehart intercepted the group to announce that lunch was served in the dining room. Charley watched her face fall at the senator's brusque dismissal as he continued on his way, Clarice in tow. "But the senator always has his lunch at this time," she said.

"Maybe later." Charley reached out to squeeze her arm reassuringly.

"Close the door," Overstreet said when she and Mark stepped into the office.

Clarice was curled up in one of the wingback chairs as if trying to disappear into the burgundy leather. She was afraid. Not for the first time, Charley wondered at the woman's extreme reaction to a situation. Perhaps she was simply high-strung. Charley could understand her feeling regret, remorse, apprehension, but not the pure abject terror she saw in Clarice's eyes. She glanced to Overstreet. Yes, he could be imposing, intimidating, but she'd never known him to be brutal. And right now, slumped behind his desk, he looked more distressed than angry. As his eyes met Charley's she could see he was also in deep, emotional pain.

"Who wants to start?" he asked. His gaze roamed across the three of them. "What the heck is going on? Clarice, what is that room?"

Clarice whimpered.

"I think it's her sanctuary," Charley said. "At least, it started that way."

"It looks like a room in a brothel!"

Clarice sank deeper into her chair.

"Let me," Charley said gently. She pulled the other wingback chair closer to Clarice's. "Tell me about Joseph Dotremont."

"Dotremont!" Overstreet's hands slammed onto the desk and he leapt to his feet. "How many men were there?"

Charley held up a hand to urge him to sit down. "Please, Senator." She returned her focus to Clarice.

"I've never met him." Clarice's voice was thin, but Charley believed her.

"You've heard of him, though?"

"Not until the night of the *vernissage*. That awful man —Monsieur Leloup—he kept asking me how I knew him."

"You didn't know Dotremont was the true creator of the *Rouge et Jaune* paintings?"

She shook her head. "Monsieur Leloup accused me of stealing them from this Dotremont person. But I didn't. I swear."

"How did you get them?"

Clarice's gaze darted to her husband and she pulled inward again.

Charley took her hands. "Look only at me." At some point, she'd have to ask Clarice about the secret room and Albert Tyson, but Charley was certain a less direct route would have better odds of yielding the answers she needed. "Tell me about the paintings."

"Albert got them. He showed up with them one day and said it would be the perfect ruse."

"Ruse for what?"

"For not going to Ottawa."

"You knew Albert when you were in Montreal?" Charley asked.

Clarice cast her eyes down as she nodded.

"You were involved with him there?"

"We were living together—as husband and wife."

"You were married?" Overstreet choked out.

"Not officially." Clarice's chin rose in defiance. "I was trying to leave him, and when I met you..."

"You used me." Overstreet ran his hands through his hair, the dishevelment adding an aura of desperation to his words. "Did you ever love me? Or was it my money you were after?"

"It wasn't your money. It was your protection I needed." She turned to Charley. "I thought if I married someone as prominent as the senator, Albert would leave me alone. But he followed me here. Threatened to expose our relationship if I didn't continue our affair."

"How did he get the paintings?" Charley asked.

"He said he'd done some work and the guy couldn't pay the full amount, so Albert took them as compensation. He said they looked like something I could do and made me pretend they were mine."

"You didn't paint anything?" Charley asked for clarification.

"Only my signature," Clarice admitted.

"Whose idea was it to steal them after the *vernissage*?"

"That was Albert's." She stared at her husband accusingly. "You were so determined to have them exhibited, it didn't matter what I wanted."

"I thought it would give you confidence," Overstreet said. "I wanted to show you off."

"I am not an ornament!"

Charley was surprised by the spark of defiance, but

then Clarice quickly cast her eyes down and sank back, as if afraid she'd overstepped.

The senator pushed his chair back. "I think I've heard enough. Charley, Detective, please leave us."

Charley turned to look at Mark who had remained standing by the entrance to the office. He shrugged and opened the door. She rose and reluctantly followed him out of the room. She looked over her shoulder at Clarice as the door closed. She hoped she'd be okay.

"How did you find out about this Dotremont character?" Mark asked.

"Grace found him."

"Of course, she did." He chuckled. "Do you think lunch is still on?"

"How can you eat after that?"

"After what? You should be celebrating. We've had a huge break in our case."

"Bigger than you think. Dotremont was here Thursday night. Mrs. Rinehart said he came to the house asking to be let in after everyone else had left."

"So, he knew his paintings were here. Do you think he gave them to Tyson or did the scumbag steal them?"

"I don't know. But given Clarice's description of the 'scumbag's' character, I suspect he took them."

"How did Dotremont know they were here?" Mark asked.

"He must have found out from Leloup. According to Lee Rothko, he was the only one who was sent a notice of the exhibition."

"And Leloup is familiar with Dotremont's work?"

"He wrote a big article praising it."

"Hmmm." Mark leaned back against the wall. "So, both

Leloup and Dotremont were still in Kingston when the paintings were stolen Friday morning."

"Could they be the men in the blue truck? We need to talk to them," Charley said.

"Good luck with that. They have no reason to talk to us." He pushed off from the wall. "We need to brief Marillo on what we've learned so far."

"Charley! Oh good, you're still here." Hal came to join them. "I think Poppy is looking for you, Detective."

"We're on our way out," she said.

"Yes, give your sister my regards, but we must be off," Mark added.

"Would you give me a few minutes, Charley?" Hal asked.

"I can't discuss the case," she said.

"That's not what I want to talk to you about." He turned to Mark. "You don't mind, do you?"

"Not at all." Mark turned to Charley. "I'll take care of what we discussed. You stay and catch up on old times."

Charley frowned as she watched Mark saunter off.

"Sorry if I interrupted something important," Hal said.

She shook off her irritation at Mark's cavalier dismissal of her. "Nothing important. What did you want to talk to me about?"

"Our future," he said solemnly and then broke into a riotous laugh. "Oh, if you could only see your face right now."

"Very funny." She swatted at his arm.

"Come sit with me in the conservatory. Are you hungry? You missed lunch. I can have Mrs. Rine—"

"No, thank you. I'm not hungry." She followed him to a long sofa that overlooked the sprawling back grounds of the

Overstreets' property. With the leaves gone, she could see right down to the edge of Lake Ontario.

"We didn't have much of an opportunity to talk, alone, at the Cannons' dinner party," Hal began. "I wanted to know how you've been faring. I mean aside from your blossoming career in journalism, how have things been for you? It can't have been easy to push on as normal after Theo's death."

"The war was hard on everyone, but we managed as well, if not better than most, I'd say." *Where is this concern coming from?*

"I had lunch with Freddie yesterday."

Ah. Of course.

"He's worried about you."

"If he's so worried, why doesn't he talk to me about it himself?" she snapped.

Hal cocked his head and sighed.

"All right, yes, I know, it's hard for him," she said.

"With all due respect, Charley, you don't know. You will never know what it was like for him—for all of us—who were over there, but especially for Freddie who spent years in a German prison camp unable to defend himself, the other prisoners, or his country."

"Do you think he will ever be able to tell me about it?"

"I wouldn't count on it. But know that he is incredibly grateful that you didn't give up on him when he came home."

"I could never..." She choked back a sob at the memory of how many times in the past two years she'd feared she'd lost her brother to the bottle.

Hal put his arm around her, and she rested her head on his shoulder. "You're a good soul, Charley. Freddie is lucky to have you in his corner."

"It's not me," she protested. "It's Gran who's held our family together."

"She is a remarkable woman, too, but don't sell yourself short."

Charley pushed off his chest and leaned back to look at him. "Are you serious about leaving Chicago and moving back to Kingston?"

Hal's eyes creased at the corners and she was drawn into their warmth. "I wasn't sure when I came home, but I think, maybe, my family needs me here. I don't know what's going on between my father and Clarice, but something is eating away at him."

"He's had a big shock today."

"It's not that. You know what it was like growing up in our family—the relationship between my parents was awful. But after he met Clarice, Dad was happy in a way I'd never seen before. But now..." He looked up at the ceiling and appeared to be searching for the right words to explain what he meant. "I don't know what it is. Something has changed in him. He's on edge, and it's not only because of what he found out today. I noticed it as soon as I got home."

"What would you do if you stayed?"

"Well, here's the thing. My father has been pressuring me for some time to throw my hat in the ring to run for a seat in the next Parliament. With my service record and government experience, combined with the Overstreet name, you know, I'll probably win."

"And I'm sure an endorsement from the senator would be a big boost, too, if that's what you want to do." Charley forced a smile of support. *Poor Dan.* Pitted against Hal Overstreet, his political aspirations didn't stand a chance.

CHARLEY STEPPED out of the elevator onto the fourth floor of the Kingston General Hospital. She hadn't been here for several months—not since Laine Black had been discharged shortly before Christmas. But for months before that, she'd been a regular visitor during her friend's convalescence. She'd come to know the staff and most of the other patients. It was the hospital's floor for the city's war veterans, those poor souls who'd suffered catastrophic physical and mental injuries defending their country's freedom. It was a miracle that her brother, Freddie, wasn't living here among them and she was grateful for that every day.

Speak of the devil.

"I didn't expect to see you here," Charley said as her brother stepped out of the common room where the soldiers congregated during the day.

"I had a meeting."

She should have known. It was a commitment to attending regular meetings of the new abstinence program sweeping the country, and the mutual support of his fellow soldiers, that enabled him to maintain his precarious sobriety.

"Are you here to see Laine?" Freddie asked.

"Yes, she called this morning." Charley had been

surprised Laine wanted to meet her on the veterans' floor rather than in the pathology wing where she usually worked. Grace had relayed the message when Charley had finally arrived at the *Trib* that morning.

She was having a slow start to her day after an unsettled night. She'd tossed and turned in bed, unable to sleep as she debated whether she should tell Dan about Hal's plans to seek the party's nomination to run in the next federal election. It felt disloyal to keep that information to herself. Not too long ago, it would never have occurred to her to do so. She would have been working right alongside him to thwart Hal's plans. But things were different between them now, and in the wee hours of the morning, she'd finally decided to leave things be. Dan wasn't her responsibility, and her involvement in his affairs, however well-intentioned, would probably be received as unwanted interference.

Additional tables had been brought into the common room and rather than playing cards, the men seemed to be intent on another task. Charley peered over the shoulder of a young man who was cutting shapes out of patterned paper. He'd amassed quite a pile of hearts of various sizes and colours.

He glanced up at her. "Hello, Mrs. Hall. Long time no see."

"Yes, it's been a while, Mr. Clarke. How have you been?"

"Keeping well, thank you." He returned to his task.

Across the table, Jake Donnelly, his brow furrowed in concentration, was using his one remaining hand to write a message. When he finished, he lowered his pen, removed the weight that was holding the paper in place, and put the page on a small pile that was building beside him. Then he took another sheet and began the process again.

Freddie scooped up a handful of Mr. Clarke's hearts and carried them to another table where two men were gluing them onto heavy brown paper that had been folded in half. Another veteran was responsible for taking one of Jake's notes, folding it into the card, and then slipping it into an envelope.

"This is quite an operation you've got going," Charley said, pulling a chair up beside Laine who was writing addresses on the envelopes.

"Isn't it wonderful?" Laine's pixie face beamed with pride. "The soldiers wanted to do something for the widows and mothers who've lost their loved ones and won't be getting a Valentine next week."

"This was their idea?" Charley felt the germ of an idea of her own forming.

"Oh yes. All theirs. We got the addresses of the widows and mothers from the city's records. And we asked some of the shops if they could donate supplies, which they happily did." She leaned back. "You know, it breaks my heart that most of these fellows won't be getting a card or anything else for St. Valentine's Day—many have been abandoned by their sweethearts and families—and yet, their thoughts are for others, making sure they're not forgotten."

"They're heroes."

"Yes, they are." Laine grinned at her appreciatively. "Grace said you wanted a copy of Albert Tyson's autopsy. I can't give you that, of course, but I can show you the results." She spoke slowly and deliberately, only hesitating slightly on the occasional word. "Let's go somewhere else. I don't want to dampen the mood with talk of death." She stood and waved Freddie over. "Can you take over for me?" she asked and at his nod of acceptance, handed him the pen.

Charley followed her out into the corridor and then

onto the elevator to take them down to the basement where Laine had a small office.

Charley found the windowless room dreary and depressing and so unsuited to the vivacious sprite-like woman Laine had been. But since her head injury, Laine found bright lights and excessive noise draining and needed the dark quiet to restore her energy.

She handed Charley a file folder from the top of her desk. "Here's the final report. A copy was sent to Detective Marillo yesterday afternoon."

Charley flipped through the pages. There were photographs of the body on the autopsy table and diagrams indicating the trajectory of the bullets. "Anything surprising?" she asked.

"Nothing. He was shot three times—one in the chest and two in the abdomen. He died almost instantly."

"Did the police ever find the bullet casings, do you know?"

Laine shook her head. "If it was a revolver..." she began and then shrugged.

"Do you know the calibre of the bullets?"

Laine leaned forward and pointed to a spot about two-thirds down the page Charley was looking at.

.45 calibre.

"It's not going to help you unless you're able to find the gun that shot them."

"Darn it!" She shouldn't have been surprised. Pretty much every man who'd served in uniform since the Boer War had a .45 calibre revolver, including her own father, whose British Bull Dog from the Great War was sitting in her family's safe. "It must have been a high-powered load, though, if it was fired from across the yard and rico—" She glanced up sharply. "Wait a second. Did *all three* bullets ricochet off the side of the house before hitting him? That's more than a lucky shot."

"I don't know where that idea of ricocheting bullets came from. Detective Marillo asked the same thing."

"He fell facing the house. If the second group of thieves shot at him from behind, but he was hit in the chest..." Charley paused as Laine cocked her head to the side, frowning. "That's not what happened?"

Laine shook her head. "The impact from the bullets likely spun him a bit as he fell, but he was certainly looking directly at the person who shot him."

"WELL, HELLO THERE, MRS. HALL." Sergeant Jerry Kearn smiled at her from behind the high information counter in the Kingston Police Department.

Charley scanned the lobby, but there was no one else there. "Detective Spadina asked me to meet him here."

"*Mister* Spadina is back in the cells with *Detective* Marillo," Kearn said. "You can wait for them in the office. I'll let them know you're here."

Charley removed her coat and hat and laid them on one of the chairs in the Sergeant's office. Mark had called her at the *Trib* as she was putting the finishing touches on her feature article for tomorrow's women's pages. She hadn't spoken to him since they'd discovered Clarice's secret room two days ago. Normally, she'd be anxious to hear how things went when he'd taken what they'd learned to the police, but since he hadn't bothered to contact her, she suspected Marillo hadn't seen the same connections they had. But a chilly response from the cops wasn't the only reason she hadn't sought out Mark. Both Jean-Philippe Leloup and Joseph Dotremont had hung up on her when she telephoned them in Montreal, and she didn't want to have to admit his prediction had been correct.

Both Mark and Marillo looked grumpy as they stalked

into the office.

"Sorry to have brought you here under false pretenses," Mark said.

"You didn't give me any pretense," she said. "Why did you ask me here? And what's wrong with the two of you?"

Marillo scowled as he pulled out the chair behind the desk and sat down. "Spadina told me what you'd learned about the paintings being done by Joseph Dotremont and that he'd been in town around the time of the theft."

"And that Leloup had to have been the one to tell him they were here," Charley added.

"Yeah, all that."

"So why the long faces? That gives us two suspects. Both with motive, means, and opportunity."

"But no proof," Marillo said.

"Then let's look for some." She turned to Mark. "We need to interview them. There has to be something to tie one or both to this."

Mark and Marillo exchanged pained glances. "We just did," Mark said.

"Did what?"

"Interview them."

"And they had nothing to say," Marillo added. "Both had alibis for the time of the thefts and claimed not to know the other was even in Kingston."

"Wait a minute!" Charley put her hands on her hips and glared at the two men. "They're here? How did you get them to come to Kingston? I tried calling them and they wouldn't even speak to me."

"Not to give offence, but I believe the police's powers of persuasion might be a little stronger than your own, Mrs. Hall. And yes, they're here. In the back." Marillo turned to Mark. "I can't keep them much longer."

"No point. We've got nothing on them," he said.

"What did they tell you?" Charley asked.

"Frankly, it's the destruction of the paintings that makes either of them seem unlikely suspects," Marillo said. "I mean, what would be the point of going to all that trouble to destroy something you'd stolen not an hour before?"

"Our initial theory that Leloup might have wanted to destroy the paintings because he thought they were an abomination to the Abstract Expressionism movement doesn't hold given what he wrote about Dotremont's work," Mark said.

"I thought we were missing something and that was why I had them come, but..." Marillo shrugged. "Dead end."

"Can I speak to them?" Charley asked.

"What would be the point of that?" Marillo asked.

"You never know. People sometimes tell me things they don't intend to."

"Mrs. Hall, if two trained police interrogators couldn't get them to confess, I sincerely doubt a reporter from the local newspaper—"

"Why not give her a shot?" Mark interrupted. "I mean, what have we got to lose?"

"It's highly irregular." Although his mouth was pursed in disapproval, Marillo's tone was hesitant.

He's starting to waver.

"Leloup doesn't like women. He always tries to show off his superiority. Maybe, in his arrogance, he'll slip up around me. Dotremont may do the same," Charley said pressing her advantage. "Or maybe having a woman in the room will soften him up? Make him feel more relaxed? Come on, Detective, you'll never know unless we try."

Marillo sighed and stood. "All right, Mrs. Hall. I'm not

convinced it will do us any good, but I'll let you have a go at them. Which one do you want first?"

"I want to talk to them together."

Marillo's eyebrows rose to the top of his head. "Of course, you do," he grumbled.

The detective led her and Mark through a locked door into the back of the police station where the cells were housed. Charley looked around, curious, as they proceeded down a long corridor, masculine murmurs penetrating through the wall on her left.

"Never been back here before?" Marillo glanced at her. "The men's cells are on that side." He pointed in the direction of the voices. "Guard room, locker room," he rhymed off motioning to doorways on the right as they passed. "Matron's office..." He paused. "Grab a couple of chairs will ya, Spadina." He picked up a wooden chair that was near the entrance himself and then continued, "Women's cells."

When they got to the end of the hallway, he opened the door to a grey, windowless room that was empty of all furniture. What little light there was came from a single, bare lightbulb hanging from the ceiling. The room was made more unpleasant by its cloying dankness and the scent of urine, which Charley attributed to the hole in the floor in the back corner of the room.

Marillo set down his chair and Mark did the same with the two he'd brought with him. "We use this room for transients. Make yourself comfortable. We'll get the suspects."

Comfortable? Here?

Was it just this room or were all the cells where the prisoners stayed equally odoriferous? She hadn't heard anything coming from the women's block when they'd passed, so she assumed they were currently unoccupied. She'd have to ask Marillo more about the women they usually held here. Maybe she could interview the matron for the *Trib*. She'd likely have some interesting stories to tell.

Charley positioned two of the chairs side-by-side against the back wall and the third facing them. She assumed Mark and Marillo would stand guard by the door—not that she expected either Leloup or Dotremont to make a break for it. They were hardly dangerous criminals.

Jean-Philippe Leloup looked distinctly out of place in a bright yellow dress shirt and dark purple pants. He wasn't wearing a scarf today, but she suspected it was police procedure to remove such items. She glanced at his waist—yup, no belt either.

Joseph Dotremont, dressed in black from top to bottom, seemed more appropriately attired as a resident of the jail.

"Thank you for agreeing to speak with me," Charley said, indicating they should sit in the chairs she'd arranged.

Leloup glowered at her. "I remember you. The reporter."

"Yes." She smiled pleasantly at him and turned to Dotremont. "My name is Charley Hall. I saw your *Rouge et Jaune* paintings. They are quite striking."

"*Merci, madame*, but if you'll excuse me, why do you wish to speak with us? I have told the police everything I know. I want to return to my home." His accent was, as Mrs. Rinehart had noted, distinct from either the French or Quebec accents she was used to.

"It was your exclusive use of two colours, the red and yellow, that fascinates me. You did the same with your *bleu et rouge* and *jaune et bleu* series. I imagine your original intention was to have them appear as a full set."

"*La collection primaire*. Twelve paintings in all."

"Each painting matched with two others in how the colours were used, even the brush strokes." Charley nodded. "The only difference being the colours of the paint. Two for each series."

"If you want a lesson in art critique, Mrs. Hall, I'd be happy to give you one *after* we are released," Leloup snapped.

"Thank you Monsieur Leloup, but I don't think that will be necessary. I read your highly informative article on the remaining two series. You didn't mention the third. Why is that?"

"I wasn't aware there was a third."

"Until you received Mr. Rothko's bulletin. And then you came to see it for yourself." She turned to Dotremont. "And you found out about it from Monsieur Leloup?" She didn't wait for a response. "Of course, you did. He was the only person to receive a bulletin."

"*Oui*, he showed me the notice and asked if someone might have copied my work."

"But you knew they were yours. Albert Tyson had taken them from you. And now you knew where they were. Interesting that you both ended up in Kingston, the night of the *vernissage*."

"Is it?" Leloup looked past her to Marillo. "What is the point of this? I have told you where I was when the paintings were stolen."

"As have I," Dotremont said.

"Mrs. Hall?" Marillo asked.

"I'm getting there, Detective." She turned back to the two suspects. "This is what has the police stymied. Even though you lied to Detective Spadina and me when we first talked to you, Monsieur Leloup, you have an alibi for the time the paintings were stolen. Both the hotel manager and bartender will swear to it. And I understand you do, too, Monsieur Dotremont."

"I was stranded in a rooming house because of the storm."

"Many witnesses, I assume." She smiled knowingly. "But it is possible either of you could have arranged for someone else to take the paintings for you."

"And set them on fire?" Dotremont stared at her incredulously, his pale complexion darkening to a deep red. "I could never..."

"And that is the point that is most troubling, isn't it?" Charley said. "Whoever took the paintings deliberately destroyed them and what possible motive could either of you have for doing that?"

"That is precisely what I have been saying," Leloup said.

"Except they weren't, were they?" Charley ignored the grunts of surprise from Mark and Marillo behind her. It was the reactions of the two men in front of her she wanted to gauge. "I mean, it *looked* like they had been burned. There were enough ash and bits of crates and canvases to indicate it was the four paintings. And I suspect that four crated paintings were burned that morning."

"But you said...please, madame, do not toy with me." Dotremont's eyes rounded and he leaned forward.

"Rest assured, monsieur, I am quite certain your *Rouge et Jaune* series is safe. Isn't that right, Monsieur Leloup?"

"This is madness." Leloup leapt to his feet. Faster than Charley thought possible both Marillo and Mark had him by the shoulders and were urging him to resume his seat. They remained standing beside him.

"You were very clever, Monsieur Leloup, in making it appear as if the paintings had been burned beyond recognition. Unfortunately, some bits of the canvases remained. Not unfortunate for the police, of course, since one of those bits had Clarice's signature, deliberate I am sure, to prove they had the correct paintings. But I say unfortunate for you because those bits also had paint on them. Green paint. A colour which could not possibly have come from the stolen artwork. The police wouldn't have known that since none of them had ever seen the paintings in full colour."

"My paintings still exist?" Dotremont asked. "Where are they?"

"Safely stored in Montreal, I would imagine," Charley said. "I suspect Monsieur Leloup was going to wait until your remaining two series achieved some degree of success and was then going to produce the 'missing' series. Perhaps claiming it was the greatest find of the decade or some such nonsense."

"Is this true?" Dotremont turned to Leloup. "Do you have them?"

Leloup threw up his hands. "All right. I give up. Yes, I have the *Rouge et Jaune*. They are perfectly safe, and I will return them to you without seeking any compensation."

"Compensation? Why would I pay you for them? They are mine!"

"A finder's fee, isn't that what they call it? You would never have recovered them if not for me. And if I hadn't taken them, you might have been embroiled in years of litigation with the Overstreets."

Oh, brother! Charley doubted Clarice would have kept up the charade if Dotremont had claimed his paintings.

Leloup looked up at Marillo. "Now that this has been resolved, may I go?"

"There's still the matter of Mr. Tyson's murder," Marillo said.

"I had nothing to do with that," Leloup countered. "The men who took the paintings said he was already dead when they arrived, and a white truck was racing away. Three of the paintings fell out of the back and the fourth had been dropped by the door."

Dotremont moaned in agony.

"And they left him there?" Marillo asked. "Stepped around him to get the last painting? What kind of men did you hire?"

"Men I trust." Leloup raised his chin defiantly. "I will give you their names so you may speak with them. I assure you, Detective Marillo, they did not do this horrible thing."

"All right. Leave me their names." Marillo rubbed his eyes wearily. "This case has been so crazy I don't know which way is up. If he doesn't return your paintings, Monsieur Dotremont, let me know and I'll have him charged."

"What? You're not going to charge him now?" Charley stared at the cop in amazement.

"I could, but it would be a nightmare to prosecute. Yes, he took the paintings from Mrs. Overstreet, but she shouldn't have had them to begin with. And while she was an accessory after the fact, it is Albert Tyson who stole the paintings in the first place, except I can't charge him because he's dead. If the paintings are back where they belong, I am satisfied. Is that okay with you, Monsieur Dotremont? You never reported the original theft so I'm thinking you'd rather forget the whole thing."

"*Oui.* Provided I have my *série rouge et jaune* back, I am content."

"I can go then?" Leloup stood, looking relieved.

"I'll have Sergeant Kearn do the paperwork. Wait here." He nodded to Mark and Charley, indicating they should leave.

Charley hesitated by the door. "Can I ask you something, Monsieur Dotremont?" She returned to stand by her chair in the centre of the room, ignoring the huff of protest from Marillo. "I thought the point of Abstract Expressionism was spontaneity—that the painting was a way to communicate what was happening subconsciously. But your collection is so precise. Each painting has not one, but two matches, perfectly identical in all but colour."

"It was an experiment to see if I could recapture the emotion of the first painting through its recreation. Like a child learning the rules of their society. Who told them what to think—what to feel—about this or that? No, they absorb it all without knowing how and once there, it is part of them."

"Which is why you chose the three primary colours," Charley said.

"*Exactement.*"

"Which came first?" she asked.

"Isn't it obvious? It's *La série rouge et jaune*," Leloup said. "I could tell as soon as I saw the images of one of the paintings reproduced in the bulletin. It's why I had to come to see the series for myself. I could feel in it a passion that the other series couldn't quite capture."

"Even though they're identical?"

Leloup and Dotremont stared back at her, their expressions a combination of contempt and pity.

No, she didn't get it. But obviously, many others did. She was tempted to ask Dotremont if he considered his experiment a failure but figured that would only open her up for more derision.

Once they were back in the Sergeant's office, Mark turned on Marillo. "Are you simply going to take Leloup's word that his men didn't shoot Tyson? That's great detective work, bub. Let's ask the perp if he's guilty. No need for an investigation or a trial—"

"Stand down, Spadina!" Marillo barked. "I know what you think of Kingston PD, but this is *my* case. There may be a thing or two you aren't aware of."

"Such as?"

"Such as the shots that killed Albert Tyson almost certainly came from the direction of the house."

"Dowden?" Mark asked. "It wouldn't be the first time a perp called the cops to try to throw them off his scent."

"I'm keeping him under surveillance, to be safe, but it's unlikely," Marillo said. "Given what we know about where the shooter was standing, it doesn't fit. No, I think we're looking at someone in the Overstreet family. I'm headed over there now."

"I want to go with you," Charley said. "You owe it to me after I solved the art thefts for you."

Marillo's face turned a shade of red Charley had never seen before and she worried she'd overstepped. As he had a habit of reminding her, it was her civic duty to aid law enforcement. He could argue that she should have told him sooner the destroyed paintings were decoys. She'd felt something was off when they'd discovered the burned canvases, but it wasn't until she'd seen the photos in the magazine article that she'd figured out what it was.

"I know the family," she said, changing tack. "I may be able to provide some insight."

Marillo turned to Mark, who shrugged. "If they close ranks, she could be an asset."

"And I suppose you think you should come, too?" Marillo blew out his exasperation. "Fine. But to be clear, this is *my* case and I'll do all the talking."

Senator Overstreet was quite amicable when Charley and Mark first arrived with Detective Marillo and four uniformed constables. But his composure faltered when Marillo asked for the keys to his office desk where he kept his firearm.

Charley sat uncomfortably on one of the armchairs in the conservatory. Marillo had only wanted the senator and Clarice to join them, but both Hal and Poppy had insisted on being present, too.

"How much longer?" Poppy glared at Charley from across the room.

Charley wasn't sure if the woman's irritation stemmed from having to wait while the police conducted a search of the senator's office or the fact that Mark had chosen a chair beside Charley rather than accepting an invitation to join her on the sofa.

Harold was seated beside his daughter while Clarice cowered in the armchair closest to the entrance where Marillo stood. Hal remained standing by the windows along the back of the room. He hadn't said a word since they arrived but the look of recrimination he gave Charley made her waver. She was about to commit the ultimate betrayal of people she'd once thought of as family. Knowing that it was in the pursuit of justice didn't make it any easier.

"You're out of your mind if you think one of us murdered that Tyson fellow," Hal said, glaring at Marillo.

"Time will tell," the cop replied confidently. "Now, I know it wasn't you, Mr. Overstreet. In fact, you are the one person who couldn't possibly have done it."

"Are you sure?" Hal shot back. "Maybe I snuck into town days before I told you I was here."

Charley heard Marillo's breath catch and she realized Hal had caught him flat-footed.

"Except that the city was in the middle of a snowstorm and all the flights from Chicago were cancelled," Charley interjected smoothly. She couldn't believe no one else had thought to check Hal's alibi. There was no way Sherman would have printed anything she'd written unless he was certain she'd fully checked all her facts—twice. "I suppose you might have been able to get through via automobile, but I spoke with the Trade Commissioner and he says even without the storm you'd have missed your flight on Thursday because you were with him in a difficult meeting with representatives of the American steel industry. And after that, the two of you celebrated into the wee hours of Friday morning."

Hal's protest of "You called my boss?" was drowned out by Poppy's accusation to her brother, "You had no intention of being here! You deliberately left me to deal with *her* alone."

"It wasn't deliberate, Poppy. We hit a last-minute snag in our negotiations." He turned to his father. "I did intend to be here to support Clarice at the *vernissage*. Truly I did."

"And what about me?" Poppy challenged Charley. "Do you think I did it?"

"I wish," Charley murmured. "No, Poppy. I don't believe it was you, either. What motive could you possibly have had? You don't like Clarice, that's not a secret, but I am quite sure you didn't know she was having an affair with Tyson before Wednesday."

"That's the first sensible thing you've said all day," Poppy said, smugly settling into the sofa.

Charley knew she shouldn't be surprised by how self-absorbed Poppy was, but it still shook her to realize how little regard she had for anyone else. If it wasn't Poppy and it wasn't Hal, didn't she realize who that left?

She glanced toward the entrance as a uniformed constable carefully handed Marillo what they'd been searching for.

Holding it gently, allowing his fingers to touch only a small part of the grip, Marillo raised the revolver to show it to the group. "Is this yours, Senator?"

"Of course. I told you it was there." Overstreet didn't try to hide his impatience.

"And you are certain you have the only key to the desk," Marillo said.

"The only one. I often have important government documents that I need to keep secure."

Marillo snapped open the gun's cylinder. "Three spent cartridges," he said.

"That's impossible. I haven't fired it in years." Overstreet was on his feet, but before he could even take a step toward Marillo, Mark had moved to block him.

"Easy, Senator." Mark urged him to sit back down.

"I suppose you're going to tell us that the Tyson fellow was shot by a .45," Hal said, calmly cool. "I suspect if you searched all the homes in Kingston—in all of Ontario, heck, the whole country even—you'd find Colt New Series revolvers in quite a lot of them. I have one myself. I can't think of a more common firearm."

"That's true. We'll check it for fingerprints anyway and compare its bullets with the ones we found in Mr. Tyson." Marillo handed the gun to the constable. He turned to the group. "Here's what we know. Mr. Tyson was shot three times by a .45—most likely a revolver since we haven't been able to locate any shell casings—from someone standing near the front entrance of this house. The senator owns a .45 that has three spent cartridges in its cylinder. And he admits he is the only person who has access to that gun."

"But why? *She* has the best motive," Poppy said pointing to Clarice. "She could have taken Daddy's keys..."

Clarice's eyes widened in panic and she looked imploringly at Marillo.

"That's very true," Marillo said. "You were desperate to escape Tyson, Mrs. Overstreet. So much so, you married the senator in the hope he would protect you. But that didn't work. Tyson followed you here."

"I wanted him gone," Clarice sobbed. "I would have done anything to get rid of him. But I didn't kill him. I swear I—"

"I couldn't understand your reaction after the paintings were stolen," Charley said earning a look of rebuke from Marillo. She continued anyway. He could thank her later. "I thought, perhaps, as an artist, you'd felt violated by the theft of something so precious. But they weren't your paintings, so it couldn't have been that. It was fear, wasn't it? You refused to see anyone—talk to anyone. And so, I wondered, what on earth did you have to be so afraid of?"

"You already said she was afraid of Tyson," Poppy said. "It's obvious she killed him and was afraid someone would figure it out."

Charley turned to her. "That might make sense, except, let's not forget that Clarice didn't want the paintings exhibited and Tyson was there that morning to 'steal' them so they wouldn't be. She needed him." Charley couldn't help it. She began to pace the room. "But this fear? I can see it in you now, Clarice. Why? We know about the paintings. We know about the affair. We know about the art studio. What other secret are you hiding?"

"Nothing," Clarice replied, her voice wavering.

"I think there is. You weren't asleep when Tyson and Dowden arrived to steal the paintings. You were watching from your bedroom window and saw someone shoot him. And that's why you're afraid."

Clarice turned to Overstreet. "I didn't say a word to anyone. I promise I didn't."

"You think I shot him?" Overstreet's eyes widened in shock.

Poppy jumped to her feet and Hal rushed forward from the back of the room. Overstreet and his children were protesting, talking over one another until Marillo dispatched a shrill whistle that silenced them.

"Now, everyone, sit back down and let Mrs. Hall finish," Marillo said.

"Am I interrupting?" Mrs. Rinehart pushed a tea wagon into the conservatory. She looked anxiously toward the senator and then back at Charley. "The senator likes his tea at four-thirty sharp."

"Quite right," Charley said. "I think we could all do with a cup of tea." She waited while Mrs. Rinehart poured out the cups for everyone, preparing each with the requested milk and sugar. She took a sip of her own, taken clear. And then the last puzzle piece slipped into place.

Oh, dear. She had it all wrong.

CHARLEY SET her teacup down on the side table and took a deep breath. She knew what had happened, but how was she going to prove it?

She turned to Harold Overstreet, who had resumed his seat but was staring at Clarice as if his whole world had been destroyed. She hated what she was about to do, but there was no other choice if she was going to get the confession they needed.

"I thought it was odd that you were stoking the fire when Detective Spadina and I came to speak to you the morning the paintings were stolen. The room was already exceptionally warm. You were wearing gloves, I remember."

"Was I?" He looked down at his bandaged hand.

"You had tried to burn something in the fireplace earlier that morning, hadn't you? That was when you scorched your fingers. When we arrived, you were adding more fuel to make sure whatever it was was well and truly gone." Charley glanced to Clarice before returning her gaze to the senator. "I suspect you were destroying something incriminating—something that connected you to Tyson."

"That's ridiculous!" Hal positioned himself behind his father, placing a hand on his shoulder.

"You knew Clarice had been having an affair," Charley said. "You told me as much when we spoke earlier in the week, although I didn't realize it at the time. You mentioned if you showed interest in something so important to her, it would prove your love, that she wouldn't need—and I thought you were about to say 'anything else', referring to her painting. But you almost said 'anyone'. Anyone else. That you would be enough. I didn't figure it out until a few days ago. It was when I asked Clarice if she knew Joseph Dotremont. Do you remember? You asked her how many men there had been, implying you knew there had been at least one other."

"I should have known better than to talk to a reporter— even one claiming to care for my family."

The criticism stung but Charley remained stoic.

Overstreet bowed his head. "Yes, I knew about Tyson. I'd found out several months ago."

Clarice gasped. "You never said anything!"

"What would you have me say? I was trying to figure out how to deal with it. I loved you..."

"So, you killed him? Was I to be next?"

"No!" Overstreet overturned the coffee table as he jumped to his feet in protest.

Mrs. Rinehart rushed forward to tidy up the mess, but Charley waved her back. Spilt tea and broken china weren't important right now.

Overstreet turned to Charley. "I'd never seen the man, in the flesh, until I found his body that morning. I swear."

"But you recognized him right away," Charley prompted.

Overstreet nodded and he sagged back down onto the sofa. "His image was seared into my mind. I'd been sent photographs of him and Clarice together. They arrived at my apartment, in Ottawa, shortly before Christmas. I didn't know what to do about it." He looked to Clarice. "I loved you so much. I didn't want to lose you, so I didn't say anything. I hoped that by showing an interest in your painting we would become closer and you would end the affair. I'm such an old fool." He swallowed heavily.

"And it was those photographs that you were burning in the fireplace that morning," Charley said.

The senator nodded but kept his gaze fixed on his wife. "Clarice, if you saw the killer, why do you insist it was me?"

"Because she didn't," Charley said. "The shooter was hidden by the roof of the carriage porch. She knew it wasn't Dowden because she could see him emerge from the entrance to the east wing, and the blue truck was pulling into the driveway when it happened, so it couldn't have been any of them."

"I didn't do it," the senator repeated. "I was in my office when Mrs. Rinehart came to tell me there'd been a commotion outside."

"Did you take the gun from your desk?" Charley asked.

"No, I never thought to."

"Just as well, I imagine," Charley said, "since it wasn't there."

"What are you saying?" Hal asked her. "Do you believe my father did it or don't you? I'm growing tired of this parlour game of yours."

"Oh, it's not a game." Charley began pacing the room again and stopped in front of Clarice. She glanced at Marillo, but he seemed content to let her proceed. "What did you do after you saw Tyson shot?"

"I took to my bed and pretended to be asleep until Harold came up to tell me about the theft."

"Do you know how long that was?"

"I don't know. I was in shock, but it felt like forever."

"Because it was," Charley said. She turned to Marillo. "It's the timing you see. We've had it all wrong."

"I'm listening." He folded his arms across his chest.

"Okay." She turned to Overstreet. "You followed your usual routine that morning, rising, and going for your morning walk as the sun was coming up. That would have been about seven-thirty. But there was that darn snowstorm and so you cut your usual hour-long walk short, returning to your office after fifteen minutes. You said your arrival flustered Mrs. Rinehart, who seemed to think she should have had breakfast prepared. But that doesn't make any sense, does it? Let's face it, you're a stickler for time, Senator, and breakfast is always served at eight forty-five. Isn't that right, Mrs. Rinehart?"

All eyes turned to the housekeeper. Charley figured all of the Overstreets had forgotten she was still in the room.

"Eight forty-five sharp," she said.

"After Mrs. Rinehart left, you said you worked for a while. What did you tell me? Maybe half an hour?"

"That's about right."

"And then she told you about the commotion. So, you'd have gone out there and found Tyson's body around say, eight-thirtyish?"

"Why are you so focused on the precise timing of everything?" Hal asked, clearly irritated.

"Because the timing *is* everything," Charley said. "Ask the senator. If he weren't always so precise, we'd never have learned the truth."

"And what is the truth?" the senator asked, sounding as irritated as his son.

"That you couldn't have killed Tyson. You weren't even in the house when he was shot. Dowden and Tyson arrived here at sunrise—the same time as you were heading out for your walk along the lake." Charley turned to Mrs. Rinehart. "It's the timing you see."

Even under her perfectly applied foundation, Charley could see the housekeeper had paled. "Go on," the older woman said.

"Mrs. Rinehart," Charley continued, "you sent the senator the photographs of Clarice and Tyson, didn't you? Although you told me you no longer did photography, I suspect if the police search the cellar, they'll find your photo developing studio has been used recently."

"So, what if I did? He deserved to know she was cuckolding him," Mrs. Rinehart fired back.

"Are you now suggesting Mrs. Rinehart killed Tyson?" Hal asked. "Make up your mind, Charley."

She ignored him. "You recognized Tyson when he got out of the truck and was helping load the paintings." Charley rested her hand on Mrs. Rinehart's shoulder. "You went to the senator's office and got the revolver you know he keeps in his desk—"

"How could I have done that? The senator has the only key," she countered.

"Please, Mrs. Rinehart, there is not a lock in this house you don't have a key to, whether anyone is aware of it or not."

"Well, what if the senator had left papers in Kingston that he needed in Ottawa—?"

"You had no right!" Overstreet shouted. "Those are state secrets. You could have put us all in jeopardy."

Mrs. Rinehart blanched at the reprimand.

"Please, continue, Mrs. Hall," Marillo said. "I'm assuming there's more."

Charley returned her focus to the housekeeper. "And

despite your protests, Mrs. Rinehart, you do, in fact, have a key to Clarice's studio. You gave yourself away when we were talking in the kitchen. I asked you about Clarice's involvement in the renovation and you said you couldn't be expected to know her mind or what passes for an art studio these days. You knew precisely what was in that room, didn't you?"

"It doesn't prove anything."

"The morning of the theft, you told Detective Spadina and me about the misspelling of the word gallery on the side of the truck, but when you answered the door to Dowden, it had already driven away and parked beside the east wing. The only way you'd have seen what was written on the side was if you'd gotten close to it, which you did when you came out to shoot Tyson. Were you thinking to pin it on his accomplice, Stan Dowden? Maybe that was why you made sure you got a good look at his truck."

The housekeeper didn't respond so Charley continued. "In any event, Dowden took off when the second truckload of thieves arrived. That was even better for you because it meant more suspects. The problem arose when you tried to return the gun to the senator's desk and found him already back from his morning constitutional. It took you a while to figure out what to do, but you went back to the office a while later—about thirty minutes, according to the senator—and told him about the commotion. While he went to investigate you replaced the gun. When he came back, he told you to telephone the police."

"No, you're wrong. I came to the senator as soon as I heard the commotion." Mrs. Rinehart seemed to have recovered some of her nerve.

"No, I'm afraid not. You see Dowden called the police, too, and your two calls came within minutes of one another.

After Tyson was shot, he'd driven home and conferred with his wife before calling the police. He figures about forty-five minutes had elapsed."

"Mrs. Rinehart?" The senator looked stunned.

"I gave everything to this family, and she was making a mockery of it all." Mrs. Rinehart squared her shoulders and raised her chin imperiously, looking every inch the lady of the house.

"You gave everything to this family, but you were prepared to let the senator hang for your crime?" Charley asked.

"He used to be a great man, but now he's nothing more than a silly old fool," she said with disdain.

"You've been in love with him for years, haven't you? It must have hurt you terribly when he married Clarice after his first wife died," Charley said gently.

"She never belonged here. I told her so the day she arrived. She would never measure up as the senator's wife." The housekeeper stood and strode regally across the room to Marillo. She held up her wrists "You may arrest me."

"I don't think handcuffs will be necessary, Mrs. Rinehart," Marillo said, clearly taken aback. He took her elbow and led her out of the room.

No one said anything for some time. Senator Overstreet was the first to recover. He stood and walked over to Clarice. She tentatively took his extended hand and allowed him to pull her to her feet. "I assume you can show yourselves out," he said leading his wife out of the conservatory.

Neither Hal nor Poppy had moved, but making a formal goodbye seemed absurd—*sorry, Gran*—so Charley got out of there as fast as she could, Mark close on her heels.

"Well, that didn't go quite the way I expected," Mark

said, slipping Charley's winter coat over her shoulders. "Are you okay? I know how fond you were of Mrs. Rinehart."

"It's too bad," Charley said, slowly buttoning up her coat. "As a child, I always thought she was too glamorous for domestic service."

"Do you think it's possible for people from two different classes to live happily ever after, so to speak?" Mark asked. "I mean, I wonder what would have happened if Mrs. Rinehart had told the senator how she felt after his first wife died."

That sounded a lot like sentimentality. From Mark?

"It wouldn't happen," Charley said with certainty. "First of all, she would never have told him. And second, I don't believe anyone in that family is capable of seeing her as anything other than the housekeeper—certainly not the senator. Which, I guess, adds further proof to your theory that we're all elitist snobs."

"Not all of you."

"Not Poppy?" she asked sarcastically.

Mark's serious expression vanished, replaced by that annoyingly patronizing grin. "Oh, she's definitely elitist."

"And yet you enjoy spending so much time with her." Charley crammed her hat down onto her head and wrenched open the door. Why did she allow Mark's infatuation with Poppy to get to her?

"You know, for all your investigative skills, you are pretty poor at figuring people out sometimes," he said, trotting after her.

"Are you saying I'm wrong?" She glared at him across the hood of his sedan. Should she get in or walk home? It was a short walk, but the sun had already set, and the temperature had fallen to well below freezing.

"She's a looker, I'll give her that. But frankly, Tiger, if I hadn't finally found the opportunity to break into that locked room when I did, I think I'd have gone out of my mind. How many conversations can a man have about cabarets, catamarans, and Cabernet."

Charley opened the passenger side door and slid inside.

Catamarans?

"I'm sorry, but I can't stay for breakfast." Charley poked her head into the dining room. "Laine asked me to stop by the hospital on my way to the *Trib* this morning."

"It's hardly 'on the way.' It's in the complete opposite direction," Bessie said.

"I can drive you if you'd like." Freddie wiped his mouth with a napkin and stood. "My classes don't start until later this morning and I thought I'd swing by for a chinwag with some of the lads. Give me ten minutes."

"Well, then, you can sit down for a cup of coffee, at least," Bessie suggested.

Charley demurred. Her grandmother hated to eat alone. She sighed, reached for the coffee urn and poured herself a cup.

"Good morning, all," Evelyn said, breezing into the dining room. "I passed Freddie on the stairs, he said something about leaving early. Is he not going to join us?"

It was very subtle and lasted a fraction of a second, but Gran's mouth tightened in distaste. Charley sympathized. As they'd gotten to know Evelyn over the past few months, she'd become more tolerable, but the fact she so clearly favoured Freddie did grate.

"Charlotte's not staying long, either," Bessie said, casting her a look of disapproval.

"Well, I guess it will be us two old birds again." Evelyn took her seat and waited while Rachel poured her tea for her and dished out a plate of eggs from the serving tray in the centre of the table. "Did they ever capture the thieves who stole those paintings you wrote about? I read on the weekend they caught the person who killed one of the thieves, but there was no mention of the artwork."

Charley had kept her word to Lester Pyne and allowed him to write the story about Mrs. Rinehart's arrest, and he'd done a perfectly acceptable job of relaying the facts as the police presented them. She'd asked Marillo to keep secret her role in solving the murder and he was happy to take full credit for it. She still couldn't reconcile the woman who'd glared at Senator Overstreet with such venom and accused him of being weak with the caring mother figure she'd adored as a child.

Lester had reported that Mrs. Rinehart had confessed and would plead guilty at her arraignment, which was being held later today. She hoped so, for the sake of the senator and Clarice. If there was no trial, they could be spared the scandal of revealing the affair. It would also save Mrs. Rinehart, herself, the embarrassment of having to admit her infatuation with her employer. But then again... *Heaven has no rage like love to hatred turned, Nor hell a fury like a woman scorned.* William Congreve's famous lines popped into her head. Were they from his tragedy *The Mourning Bride?* She'd have to ask Freddie. He'd know. In any event, she hoped it would all be resolved quietly—well, as quietly as a murder conviction could be resolved in this town.

"It turns out the murder and theft weren't connected." Charley crossed her fingers behind her back before adding,

"I don't imagine they'll ever find the people who stole the paintings."

"How sad for Mrs. Overstreet," Evelyn said. "And a loss for the art world if the rumours of their significance are true. I wish I had seen them for myself. You are extremely fortunate, Charlotte, to have been one of the very few people in the world to have done so."

Fortunate for Dotremont and Leloup, you mean.

When *La collection primaire* was finally exhibited publicly, there would be very few who could question the addition of *La série rouge et jaune.* Lee Rothko would stay quiet, too, no doubt relieved he'd narrowly escaped the notoriety of exhibiting stolen artwork.

"Are you ready?" Freddie called from the doorway. "Whoa!" He stepped back to allow Rachel, carrying an enormous bouquet of roses, to pass. He followed her into the dining room. "What have we here?" He snatched the notecard as Charley accepted the bouquet. "Mrs. Charlotte Hall."

Charley wrinkled her nose at the sweet fruity perfume that enveloped her as she placed the bouquet onto the table. She turned to her brother. "Give that to me!"

Freddie grinned broadly as he handed the card to her. "A secret admirer, perhaps? It is St. Valentine's Day."

"They're absolutely lovely," Evelyn said. "A dozen pink roses for admiration and a dozen red roses for love—or the promise of it."

Charley opened the card, trying to ignore the crimson flush she knew was staining her cheeks. "They're from Hal Overstreet. He's an old friend who's come back to town," she added for Evelyn's benefit.

"I don't remember you and Hal being all that close

when you were younger," Gran said. "He's quite a bit older. Didn't he used to babysit you and his sister?"

"That was a long time ago, and he's not all that much older." It was only flowers, for heaven's sake. But she knew the reason for Gran's concern. Bessie had always believed Charley's relationship with Dan Cannon was doomed because of his political aspirations; it was unlikely she'd be optimistic about a union with Hal Overstreet. Her grandmother simply did not want to see her heart broken again.

"I had lunch with Hal the other day," Freddie said. "We talked about you mostly. He seemed to think that since I'm the man of the house, he needed to seek my permission to ask you out."

"He did what?" Charley stared at her brother askance.

"Oh, don't worry, I put him straight." Freddie grinned as his gaze took in the expressions of the three irate women staring at him. "I said the women in our household are intelligent and independent, and quite capable of determining if and with whom they wish to consort, without any interference from me."

"Oh bravo," Bessie said, applauding him.

"Chin chin." Evelyn raised her teacup in a toast.

Charley threw her arms around her brother and buried her head into his shoulder. She felt tears prickling behind her eyes as her heart swelled with love and gratitude for the man who'd fought so hard to come back to them.

"I also told him that if he breaks your heart, I will rain hellfire down on him the likes of which he's never seen," Freddie whispered in her ear.

FREDDIE DROPPED Charley off at the door of Kingston General Hospital and drove off to find a parking spot. It was teeming rain outside. If the prediction of the weatherman held true, the nine inches of snow that fell a little over a week ago would be gone by the end of the day.

"Charley!" Grace waved at her from across the lobby.

"I didn't expect to see you here," Charley said, approaching her friend.

"Laine asked me to come, too. I thought I'd wait down here for you and then we could go upstairs together."

"Okay. Freddie should be only a moment. Do you know what this is about?"

Grace shrugged. "Look!" She pointed toward a group of three—two men and a woman—who had entered the waiting area. "The bigwigs are here. That's the president of the hospital, and the man in the white lab coat is the chief surgeon. And is that....?"

"Clarice Overstreet," Charley confirmed as the woman made a beeline toward them.

She looked far better than the last few times Charley had seen her. Clarice's pale hair was fashionably tamed by pin curls and her hazel eyes were bright—it was only if you looked closely that you could see her carefully applied foundation was hiding the bluish remnants of her recent anguish.

"I'm so glad I ran into you," Clarice said after Charley had introduced her to Grace. "I know how fond you are of Harold and his family. I wanted to let you know that he and I spent the whole weekend talking and we're going to make a go of our marriage. In fact, that's why I'm here. I've volunteered to join the board of directors for the women's auxiliary at the hospital. It's a start, but a senator's wife needs to set an example for the community." She flushed and looked down, running her hand over the brown-checked skirt of her dress. "I do care for him, you know. And maybe in time..." She glanced up as if seeking Charley's blessing.

"I wish the best for the both of you," Charley said.

"I was also hoping... Well, since Hal has decided to move back to Kingston, I expect we'll be seeing a lot of you—at least when Harold and I aren't in Ottawa. I was hoping, maybe, we could become friends."

"I don't know how much of Hal I'll be seeing, but I would like us to be friends," Charley said determined to quash any rumours before they had a chance to run rampant.

"Who's Hal?" Grace asked her after Clarice left them.

"That's a story for another day," Charley said. "Oh, look, here's Freddie. Shall we go up?"

The veterans' floor was a hive of activity as they stepped off the elevator. There were more than the usual number of people milling around—not only patients and nurses but community members, too. Cards decorated with Valentine's hearts were tacked up all along the walls, and a table was overflowing with cookies, pies, and cakes. The common room erupted in applause as they entered, and those men and women who could stand on their own rose to their feet.

"Isn't it marvellous?" Laine said moving as quickly as she could to embrace Charley. "And it's all because of you."

Charley peered over Laine's head and mouthed *"What's going on?"* to Grace and Freddie who were beaming at her.

"It started Saturday, right after the *Trib* published your article about the Valentine's Day cards the veterans were sending to the widows and mothers," Grace explained.

"It's been non-stop ever since," Laine said, releasing her. "People have been dropping off baked goods, cards, letters, games—all kinds of treats to show the soldiers they've not been forgotten."

"The power of the press!" Freddie proclaimed. "Nice to see it being used for good, for a change."

"I had no idea." The room seemed to sway, and her head felt as if it was floating off her body. Maybe she shouldn't have skipped breakfast. She plucked a cookie off a tray and joined one of the groups of veterans.

For the next hour, she wandered from group to group, chatting easily with the men, all of whom were effusive in their gratitude. She felt embarrassed by their appreciation. They were the heroes, not her. It shouldn't take an article on the women's pages for the city to remember that.

"I was told I'd find you here."

She turned to see Mark approaching her from the elevators. His trilby hat was dripping water onto the shoulders of his already drenched overcoat.

"I take it the rain hasn't let up," she said. "What are you doing here?"

"I told you, I came to see you." From behind his back, he produced a somewhat battered flowering plant. "Happy St. Valentine's Day."

She'd never seen anything like it. Orange flower petals, speckled with dark spots, curved backward on top of gracefully arching stems. And at the centre of each bloom extended six long slender stalks capped by a velvety bud.

"It's a tiger lily," Mark said. "Sorry, it got a little banged up with the rain and wind today."

"It's beautiful." She wondered if the coded colours of roses applied to other plants. Surely not. Or if they did, she doubted Mark would be aware of the Victorian-era symbolism. Orange, after all, was said to be the colour of desire.

She felt the flush race up her cheeks. "I need a glass of

water, it's terribly warm in here," she said to try to cover her embarrassment. "Thank you for the plant. It's very thoughtful."

"I didn't want you to feel left out now that Cannon's married," he said. "Let's face it, Tiger, no one else is likely to give you flowers."

She should have known better. Charley turned on her heel and stomped off, sorely tempted to drop the plant in one of the garbage bins she passed on the way to the nurses' station at the far end of the hallway.

"Oh, how lovely," Grace said, picking up the pot Charley had slammed down onto the counter. "I've seen pictures of these. Mark must have gone to a great deal of trouble to get this for you. I don't imagine you can buy them from a regular flower shop."

"I can't imagine he went to any trouble at all," Charley said. "I don't understand him one bit. On the one hand, he does something nice, like buying me flowers—or a hair comb —and then he makes some snide comment that robs the gesture of any sense of..." What was the word she was looking for? Kindness? Fondness? Amity? She gave up. "I don't know."

"He likes you."

"He barely tolerates me."

Grace giggled as she placed the pot on the counter. "No truly. Mark is like the little schoolboy who likes the girl in his class, but he doesn't know how to tell her, so he pulls on her pigtails. For the two of you, though, it's not pigtails. It's verbal sparring. He's been alone all his life, Charley. He doesn't know how to express his feelings for you."

Charley turned to look back down the hallway. Mark was talking with Freddie. For a fraction of a second, she imagined him asking her brother for his permission to ask her out.

No, Mark would never do that. Not because it was old-fashioned or a custom of the moneyed classes he liked to disparage. He wouldn't do it because he truly knew her. Perhaps it came from being an orphan and having to become self-reliant at a young age, or from his experience as a police detective, but somehow Mark understood her in a way very few people did. He wasn't threatened by her desire for independence, which she found refreshing. At the same time, he wasn't afraid to challenge her beliefs. And while she'd never admit it to him, she liked that. It could be exhausting, but it made her a better person.

Their relationship was prickly, to be sure. No one got under her skin as he did. But Charley gave as good as she got, so who was pulling whose pigtail?

Mark raised his gaze and stared directly at her. A self-satisfied smile appeared, arrogantly acknowledging he knew she'd been watching him. She returned it with a scowl, which only broadened his grin.

She turned to Grace. "We'd better get to the *Trib*." She picked up the tiger lily. "Sherman is probably having kittens wondering what's happened to his crackerjack researcher and ace reporter."

She wasn't going to let Mark's cockiness get to her, she decided, resolving to take pleasure in the gift alone.

Charley and Grace made their goodbyes to Laine, the nurses and the veterans as they headed to the elevator. To Mark and Freddie, she called out a breezy "See ya later, alligator," as she strutted past.

She could feel Mark's eyes following her, but she didn't feel the need to turn around to catch him at it. Let him wonder. After all, she could give as good as she got.

A death behind a locked door. An unexpected ice storm. What has Charley gotten herself into now?

The trip to a lakeside resort was to be her fresh start until a suspicious death threatens not only her budding romance but all of their lives.

Can Charley can solve the puzzle or will she end up with a failing grade, trapping them with a devious killer? Get *Schooled in Murder* to learn the answer.

Want more from Charley and her friends? Head over to my website (www.BrendaGayle.com) and sign up for the *Gayle Gazette* to keep up-to-date on new releases, exclusive access to special features and giveaways. Plus, you'll get a free download of a solve-it-yourself *Bessie Stormont Whodunit*. Yup, Gran has some real detective skills, too.

HISTORICAL NOTES

As the COVID-19 pandemic continues into 2021, my ability to visit the national archives to research local newspaper articles from the period covered in the story has been curtailed. So, once again, it's Google to the rescue.

ABSTRACT EXPRESSIONISM IN CANADA AND *LES AUTOMATISTES*

Since the 1920s, artists in English Canada have been heavily influenced by landscape painting, most famously that of the Group of Seven. Modernist movements, such as Cubism, Surrealism and Abstract Expressionism were often viewed as subversive by the Canadian public and the acquisition of such works by public galleries was invariably a source of controversy. And still is.

In Quebec, a modernist collective known as *Les Automatistes* began having exhibitions in the early 1940s; however, its artistic influence was not felt much beyond Montreal. Like the Group of Seven, its members were looking to create a distinctively Canadian artistic identity.

Les Automatistes favoured a fluid, painterly technique over the comparatively reserved, hard-edged abstraction that was popular in the U.S. and Eastern Europe at the time.

WEATHER DATA

Weather is a Canadian obsession. We love to talk about it, complain about it, and compare worst weather stories. Fortunately, several government databases cater to this national pastime and provide historical records of daily high and low temperatures and precipitation for major cities and regions across the country. It is fact that a major storm moved into Kingston on the evening of Thursday, February 3, 1949, depositing about nine inches of snow before it was done Friday afternoon. Similarly, over an inch of rain fell on February 14 of that year, washing most of it away, which must have made for a rather challenging Valentine's Day.

A CHARLEY HALL MYSTERY, BOOK 6

IN ANOTHER CORNER of the room, Charley spotted Dan and Meredith. "I'm just going to go say hello to Dan Cannon and his wife," she said, excusing herself. As she approached, she saw the couple was already engaged in conversation with an older, seated, man. He had shaved off his trademark beard sometime in the decade since she'd last seen him, but Charley recognized Foster Bennett's wispy grey hair and the round spectacles that enlarged his hazel eyes to give them an owl-like quality. She hesitated to interrupt them and wondered if Freddie would mind if she joined his group.

"Hello, Mrs. Hall—Charley, I mean."

She recognized the softly accented voice and took a calming breath before she turned toward it. "Colin," she said, acknowledging Dan's political backer and campaign manager. "I'm surprised to see you here. Are you hoping to still drum up support for Dan's nomination? Or perhaps convince Hal to step down?"

His smile looked as forced as hers felt. "No, this is purely a social visit. No politics involved."

"You must be disappointed that Dan didn't get the party's nomination, though." She didn't know why she was needling him. She'd never liked or trusted Colin Banks, but they'd agreed to a truce—for Dan's sake—some months ago. She knew it was too much to hope that with Dan's political aspirations dashed, Colin would disappear from all their lives. After all, he was still Meredith's brother.

"You should ask Dan about that. Although, I do have to wonder about your loyalty to our good friend. Is it your intention to rub his nose in his defeat by arriving on the arm of his political rival?"

"It's not like that. Dan knows Hal and I are old friends. I had no idea he was even going to be here."

Colin shrugged. "If you say so."

Charley opened her mouth to argue her point but was cut off by Foster Bennett clearing his throat as he rose to his feet. She turned her back on Colin and nodded a silent greeting to Dan and Meredith as they joined them.

"Greetings to you all and welcome to the Bennett Family Resort. I am sorry I haven't yet greeted you all individually, but I promise I will make it up to you tomorrow. Right now, 'To all, to each, a fair good-night, and pleasing dreams, and slumbers light.'" He waved his arm and bowed deeply before turning on his heel and marching from the room.

"Well, that was rather abrupt, but very typical for Old Benny, wouldn't you say, Cannon?" Hal had joined their group. "Who was that he quoted? Walter Scott, I think." He turned his back on Dan. "Meredith, it is lovely to see you again. My stomach still rumbles with pleasure whenever I remember the wonderful onion tart you served at dinner a few months ago."

"Thank you." Meredith beamed at him. "Mrs. Harper, our housekeeper, is a genius in the kitchen."

"You are very fortunate, indeed," Hal said.

"I didn't expect you to be here," Charley whispered to Dan while Hal and Meredith continued to exchange pleasantries.

"Why ever not?"

"You never had Mr. Bennett for English class."

"Neither did you and yet, here you are."

"I'm here as a guest of Hal's. And Freddie's," she added quickly.

Dan quirked an amused eyebrow at her. "Let me guess: Freddie is supposed to be some sort of chaperone to appease your grandmother?"

"Something like that." She scowled at him and then softened her glare. "I'm sorry you didn't get the party's nomination to run for Parliament in the next election. I really didn't come with Hal to tweak your nose over it."

Dan blinked several times and shook his head slightly. "The thought never occurred to me." He frowned. "It's politics, Charley. You know nothing is certain. Besides, it's probably better that I spend a few more years as an alderman anyway. Although..." He cocked his head and grinned. "I may consider running in the next provincial election if I get the opportunity. I'd love to kick those Tories out of power."

His expression turned serious again and he took Charley's arm to draw her away from the group. "Look, I know I have no right to interfere in your love-life—"

"It's not like that!"

"Be that as it may, but as your friend—as someone who cares very much about you—please be careful of Hal Overstreet."

"Careful of Hal? Why? What—"

But Hal and Meredith had stopped their conversation and were looking curiously in their direction.

"Trust me," Dan whispered before returning to his wife.

Want to read more? Get *Schooled in Murder*, book 6 in the Charley Hall historical mystery series.

ABOUT BRENDA GAYLE

I've been a writer all my life but returned to my love of fiction after more than 20 years in the world of corporate communications—although some might argue there is plenty of opportunity for fiction-writing there, too. I have a Master's degree in journalism and an undergraduate degree in psychology. A fan of many genres, I find it hard to stay within the publishing industry's prescribed boxes. Whether it's historical mystery, romantic suspense, or women's fiction, my greatest joy is creating deeply emotional books with memorable characters and compelling stories.

Connect with me on my website at BrendaGayle.com & sign up for *The Gayle Gazette,* my newsletter, to keep up-to-date on new releases, exclusive access to special features, giveaways, and all sorts of shenanigans. And don't forget, as a subscriber, you'll get a free download of a *Bessie Stormont Whodunit.*

Until next time...